KNOW YOUR ENEMY

TASMAN ANDERSON

ODYSSEY
BOOKS

Published by Odyssey Books in 2015
ISBN 978-1-922200-38-9

www.odysseybooks.com.au

A Cataloguing-in-Publication entry is available from the National Library of Australia

ISBN: 978-1-922200-38-9 (pbk)
ISBN: 978-1-922200-39-6 (ebook)

1
The Beginning

Silverlake was a total suckfest of a town.

Everyone knew everyone there, so spending every day seeing the same people and talking about the same things was painful, especially when the most common phrase was "I could've been something once".

I swear if you googled the definition of a soul-sucking small town, you'd find Silverlake smack bang in the middle of a blog about multi-coloured gnomes and a depressing song by John Mellencamp.

I mean, sure, Silverlake wouldn't be so bad if you liked Friday night bingo, annual town festivals, and being called anything but your actual name, but that just wasn't me.

My name isn't Nicky, or blossom, or *darling* as everyone insisted on calling me.

It's Nicole.

Just Nicole, or Nic for my friends and family.

My goal in life is to live it up in Los Angeles and kick major butt as a crime journalist. But none of that was going to be possible in Silverlake, especially since I was still stuck in high school.

I walked to school as I did every morning, through Merchant's Alley, bordered by the same, boring family-built businesses and the same shoppers, out buying the same things, wearing the same clothes. With my brain on autopilot, strolling idly along to the sound of my own footsteps, I nearly missed the custard yellow posters plastered on every surface.

"Hey, loser!" Libby waved the crumpled yellow paper in my face. "Have you seen this absolute pile of gold?"

How could I have forgotten that the new mall was opening in Bellvale soon, another hell-hole forty-five minutes from here? The poster said it was going to be the biggest thing our towns have ever seen, and they were probably right.

"Well it's official." I gave her a quick hug, rolling my eyes at her strong vice-like grip. "Today's going to suck hardcore."

I wished my parents hadn't chosen today to stay home for another discussion about our "financial situation", whatever that meant. I never wanted to skip school as much as I did in that moment.

"Why so bitchy?" she said, pulling her phone from her side pocket. "You know that everyone's going to forget that second rate tourist trap the moment someone from our soccer team figures out they're a fabulous ten on the gay scale … And let's be honest, that's pretty much guaranteed in this town."

"Tell me why you're my best friend, again?"

"Because you love that I can read you perfectly and that I can beat anyone in a diva-off."

That was Libby, all right. People would probably like her more if she wasn't borderline offensive and unapologetic most of the time. Of course, I appreciated the inappropriate jokes and snarky comments that come with being friends with Libby Michaels.

She kept tapping on her phone's keyboard, no doubt checking Facebook for the millionth time that morning.

"We're going to be late."

"Calm down, Grandma." She gave me her signature eye roll and continued the walk towards school, leaving me to trail behind her. "You know, seeing this mall for ourselves might not be such a bad thing."

When I didn't reply, she unfolded the crumpled poster and gave it a quick scan.

"Maybe we could even try for a five finger discount while we're at it."

A what? She couldn't actually mean what I thought she meant.

"My god, I can hear your brain literally freaking out." Libby laughed even as she went back to her phone and typed at hyper speed.

"You're nuts, you know that?" I said, walking ahead of her.

She caught up with me and looped her arm through mine.

"I'm not stealing anything," I added.

"Just think about it, yeah?" She tightened her grip on my arm and steered us into the front gates of Sterling High. "With your brains and my skill we can have whatever we want."

I was so caught up in our conversation, I hadn't realised we had arrived at school.

We walked through the main entrance. Although it looked more like a fortress than a school, there was a sort of cold beauty in its stonewashed concrete and the huge, crisp shapes of the letters above the soaring front door. I grabbed a quick look at them as I was carried along on the wave of 300 other chattering students, all checking their phones or checking each other out.

I hurried past the crowded junior block on my way to my second home, the library.

"Oh my god, how do you even stand to be in this place all the time? It's so dull." Libby had lagged behind me, delayed by talking to almost everyone we passed or dealing with the constant binging coming from her phone.

"Shut up, you know why I'm here," I whispered in the almost silent hall. "Stop dissing my turf."

I practically lived in the library now that applications for early admissions to Murdoch University would be opening in just a month.

"Only the brightest people go to Murdoch, and out of all of them only a select few are granted early admission." I rattled off the same answer I gave every time she made a comment. "I'm going to be one of those select few if it kills me."

I was willing to give up my senior year to study journalism from the best in the industry if it meant Los Angeles was in my future.

"Yes, yes. We all know you're going to be the Beyoncé of the print world." She waved me off. "And it looks like your favourite person is here."

I didn't have to look to know who she was talking about. Probably the only thing out of the ordinary in this town was Aiden Campbell. His amber coloured eyes would constantly change from light to dark every time I saw him. His curly dark hair framed his face perfectly and his slightly triangular shaped eyebrows accentuated his cocky smirk. Everything about Aiden made me want to find the most obscure spot I could and hide there until after graduation.

"Good lord, would you just make out with him already?"

I narrowed my eyes at Libby. "What are you talking about?"

"Don't even try to pretend with me, Sunshine." She nudged me slightly, grinning.

I honestly couldn't tell you why or when she started calling me that. I didn't exactly have a sunny disposition when it came to Libby.

"I could feel the sexual tension between you two all the way from home."

Aiden was lounging on a small bench beside the library with some tall, bulky kid in his grade. I'd never seen the two of them talk before, but the tall guy had the kind of over-eager look on his otherwise thuggish face that people got when they talked to Aiden. They were always so grateful that someone popular would have time for them at all. Aiden had this weird power about him, making him popular without having to be on a sports team.

Pathetic. I tried to forget the nagging memory that I had once been desperate for him to like me, too.

"Don't you just love how that leather jacket is clinging to all the right places?" Libby wasn't going to let this go. "Nicden, Nad, Aidcole, Aidcky …"

"What are you doing, weirdo?"

"I'm just trying to work out what your couple name would be." A grin broke across her face. "I'm leaning towards Nicden; it just sounds like the reject cousin to Nicorette."

She laughed when she saw the scowl on my face. This kind of thing was the only time I ever disliked Libby. She knew exactly what to say to push me. She knew how much I wanted to pretend Aiden never existed, and yet she kept going. Aiden and I had been friends at primary school, back when popularity didn't matter and it wasn't a problem for a boy to be just friends with a girl without rumours being spread around. High school had changed all of that.

I was ready to bolt, away from Libby's teasing and away from Aiden. But I must have moved too quickly because he noticed me.

"Well if it isn't Nicky Never Been Kissed." His eyes twinkled at the nickname. "Going to let me finally take care of that?"

The tall boy, who looked a little bit like Garrett Hedlund now that I'd had a closer look, snickered and high-fived his friend.

"You disgust me." I scowled at Aiden, letting my anger radiate toward him. He knew how much I hated being called Nicky, and yet he did it just to get a reaction.

"Is that so?" Aiden pushed himself up from his slouched position. "Or are you afraid I might just drop you again?" The first week in this hell-hole of a school, we did a trust-building exercise—and Aiden dropped me on my butt, on purpose.

"Please, the only thing you could catch is an STI," I sneered.

I could still feel the sting of hitting the concrete floor, while everyone laughed.

"You were heavy."

"Oh my god, I was not." My face flushed in a weird mixture of anger and embarrassment. "You just couldn't deal with your new friends making kissing noises at us."

"It's not my fault that they knew how badly you wanted to kiss me." His eyes shifted to my lips and his pupils widened until only a thin circle was left of his hazel irises. "Don't you want to see what you've been missing out on?"

I crossed my arms against myself and scoffed. "Please, I'm sure when I do have my first kiss, it'll be with someone who doesn't dress like they just stepped out of a 1950's gangster film."

The comment slipped out of my mouth without checking with my brain first. Instead of the snappy comeback I'd think of seconds later, I had just confirmed to my tormentor that I was, indeed, unkissed.

Colour burned in my cheeks when I saw his expression change to surprise. He was actually supposed to be my first kiss back at camp but his friends got in the way. Now he knew how much of a loser I really was. I was most likely the only girl in the entire history of the school who'd made it to sixteen without even one tiny peck on the cheek.

The morning bell saved me from further embarrassment and I quickly sidestepped the boys. I walked into the safety of my beloved library, not even waiting to wave goodbye to Libby as she sped off to her first class.

Thank god for study periods.

I slipped into the library's computer room, waving at my economics partner, Romeo, before sitting at an empty table. He smiled brightly and turned back to Kane and Denis. Together, they were the leaders of Sterling High's self-proclaimed "cool crowd".

I pulled my math textbook from my bag. There was something about trying to figure out the correlation of a statistic that made me forget about everything but the equation.

I tried not to jump when I spotted Aiden leaning on the door frame to the computer room. We shared the same study period but I never saw him in here.

"Come to have another go at me, have you?" I sighed, continuing to try to focus on my work. "Was this morning not enough?"

Silence filled the room but I refused to look his way. After this morning, the last thing I needed was Aiden turning my peaceful hideout into a fight for dominance.

Aiden cleared his throat, finally breaking the quiet tension. "You know, you really should be careful."

"And why would that be, Aiden?"

I tensed and stopped writing when I felt him move behind me. He placed his hands on either side of the desk, trapping me with his body. Aiden leant down until he was close enough to whisper in my ear.

"You've spent so much time in here that I don't think you have any fun left in you." He placed his hand on my shoulder and brushed my hair to the side. "What happened to the girl who was first in line when we went laser tagging for my 10th birthday?"

My jaw tightened and my stomach clenched painfully. We weren't kids anymore and none of that made up for how he was acting now.

Pushing my chair out, I rose from the desk, forcing Aiden to take a step back. I spun around to face him, heat rising up the back of my shirt.

"I'm exactly the same," I spat, scrunching my fists tightly until my fingers went numb. "You're the one who decided you were too cool to hang out with someone like me."

"Oh, and it's my fault you never leave this place to join the living?" he replied, regaining his composure. "Face it, you don't have a clue about real fun." He smirked and bowed his head to stare directly into my eyes. "You're exactly like everyone else in this town."

Without another word, he turned around and walked smugly out the door.

I stood in the middle of the room, my body vibrating with anger. Aiden had some nerve talking to me like that. We may have been close when we were little but he didn't know me anymore. He knew nothing about why I didn't go to parties or why I avoided the usual stupid high school stuff. If he wanted to be a walking cliché, then fine. I wasn't that pathetic.

He still knew how to push me though. We may not have been friends for a while but he was still able to get me fired up, and not in a good way. He knew mentioning Silverlake would rip at my mind, making me question whether I was really like the rest of the people here.

Maybe he was right. How was I supposed to sell an action story when I had never experienced anything that pumped me full of adrenaline? How was I supposed to write a story full of heartache when I had never felt it for myself? There was only one answer.

I couldn't.

Los Angeles was never going to happen if I continued to hide away in the library and avoid everyone.

I watched Aiden walk out of the library and instantly relaxed. Hastily, I shoved my notebook into my shoulder bag just in time for the lunch bell. It was time to do something so completely wild that it would show everyone—especially Aiden—that I wasn't boring like the others.

I pulled my mobile phone from my pocket and dialled Libby's number.

She answered after two rings. "Hello, Sunshine, finally surfacing from your textbooks?"

"I can't believe him, Libs! He thinks just because we used to be friends that he knows me. Well, he doesn't. Why can't he just leave me alone and stop making out like he's better than all of us. You know what? I'm going to teach that douche a lesson …"

"Whoa, calm your tits. What on earth are you going on about? Is this about Aiden again? I told you I was sorry." I could hear her unzipping her bag and tossing her books haphazardly inside.

"Actually, you never did say you were sorry."

"Details, details."

"Never mind that," I retorted, determined to follow through with my decision before I had a chance to chicken out. "Is it too late to take you up on that shopping trip? I think it's time I try something new."

"Well it's about bloody time," she replied. "Meet me out the front of school after class and we'll go together. Don't you dare flake on me."

With the click of the line ending our call, I left for my next class with an extra weight in my stomach.

2
Five Finger Discount

I stood in front of the mall and stared up with a mix of apprehension and excitement at the looming building. Bellvale Mall was nothing like the obscenely bright posters had made it out to be. The inside of the mall was teeming with tiny stores and traces of fresh paint mixed with the scent of roasting coffee and fried food.

Libby stood next to me and put her arm around my shoulder. "Okay, mastermind, now what?" she said, looking to me to come up with the plan, as usual. Honestly, the number of times I had to work out how to pull off her ideas would even shock Einstein.

I scanned the walkway from one side to the other. We had come in through the second entrance, right into the main food court. Just like in the rest of the mall, this section included several multi-coloured shops, all with ridiculous names.

Of course Dreamland, the mattress and bed linen store, would be painted a baby blue and covered in three-dimensional clouds. And naturally Magic Mayhem would have a monstrous black and white top hat with a rabbit jumping out of it as their logo. The only place that was actually cool was the arcade, Kapow! Its neon yellow sign looked like it came directly out of an old comic book and the sound of pinball and racing car machines carried throughout the food court.

Seriously, who named these places? Only a kid would give a store a cheesy name and then make it even more cringe worthy by decorating it with the most obvious and tacky choices imaginable.

"Okay, so I googled the new centre's directory in class so I could work out our game plan," I whispered in the crowded mall, pulling out my diagram from my bag. "We have to make sure that we get in and out within five minutes before they notice us, so I think we need to choose our targets carefully."

I didn't even get the chance to unfold the piece of paper before Libby snatched it from my hands and tore it up.

"Screw that." She grabbed my hand and dragged me to a hippie style store with the strong scent of burning incense seeping through the entrance. "This'll work."

God, she really didn't think anything through. If we were going to do this then we needed to be smart about it.

"Just stop." I ripped my hand out of her grasp and guided her away from the store. "You have no idea what kind of security system they have in place, and besides, the sales assistant is on floor duty by the look of it."

The thin man with dreadlocks roamed through each aisle, chatting with the few people looking through the racks of tie dyed scarves. We weren't going to get two steps inside that store without the man jumping on us.

"Fine, tell me then, Sherlock, which one of these stores do you suggest?" Libby flicked her hair out of her eyes.

"GroovyGirl is our best option." I pointed past the long line of shops to the tiny store with a bright purple window display. "It's pretty small and the sales assistant seems distracted. It'll be a good place to practise."

Libby raised her eyebrow but quickly relented, walking over to the store. "GroovyGirl, huh?" She shook her head and scrunched up her face in disapproval. "I dare you to find a lamer name."

GroovyGirl was lined from one end to the other with coloured jewellery. There seemed to be a different shape and colour on every single hanger. Libby walked towards the green jewellery section without any hesitation. Unsure of where to go next, I decided to go for the make-up display in the middle of the store. The rectangular stand perched on the bench held neon coloured eye shadows and different shades of lipstick. I wasn't really paying much attention to what colours I wanted; I was more focused on discreetly watching the sales assistant. She looked to be in her early twenties and had a wide smile plastered on her face. Currently she was absorbed in a conversation with some unshaven creep who seemed to be flirting with her, if you could even call it that.

"Darling, I've never seen eyes quite like yours," I heard him say to her in a strong German accent. "I could lose myself in them for days and never return."

I sneered at her girlish giggle. This was going to be much easier than I thought. Regardless, my mind seemed to go in one direction and my hands went in the other. I was having doubts for the tenth time that day. Was I really going to do this, all to prove a point? I knew it wasn't logical but my hands had other ideas. I reached out and lightly brushed my fingers over the lipsticks. My thumb caught on a blood red stick and I quickly laced my fingers around it.

My heart pounded erratically now that I was clutching the lipstick in my fist. I could feel my stomach doing acrobatic flips while every nerve in my body twitched and buzzed.

For once, I felt alive. The world had hit the slow motion switch and I was the only one still moving fast. I wasn't sure if I loved this feeling or if it scared me to death. This was a high, sure, but what happened when—if—I hit the low? What would happen to my perfectly planned life if I got caught?

I swallowed thickly and pushed the question aside; I'd work it all out later. I needed to stay focused.

With one last look at the sales assistant, I slipped the lipstick into the front pocket of my bag and walked out of the store.

* * *

"How'd you go?" Libby questioned after joining me a few minutes later.

"I took a lipstick." I put my hand in my bag, touching the sleek metallic tube. "It's red, just like a ruby."

"Finally showing off your inner devil, are we?" Libby smirked, laughing lightly.

"How about you then, Winona?"

"Take a look for yourself." She threw the bag at me. I accidentally fumbled it and glared half-heartedly at her. Inside the lining were three neon lipsticks and two mosaic patterned necklaces that I could definitely see her wearing with her school uniform.

Holy cow! How did she manage to get so much in the little time we had?

"Jealous, are we?" she said when she saw the look on my face. "So, where to next?"

"I hardly think stealing one lipstick makes me a compulsive thief," I quipped.

"Not yet, but we'll pop your klepto cherry soon enough."

I poked her in the side and exhaled loudly. Why did I have a feeling that Libby enjoyed this way more than she should?

"DIY Corner looks like a good option." I gestured towards the store that was covered in neon paint splatters, doing my best to ignore the dull ache in my stomach. "You can see this place has cameras, so we need to team up for this one."

The second I walked into the store, I felt my hands shake in excitement. DIY Corner was packed with top-of-the-line craft supplies: paintbrushes made with real horsehair, handmade canvases, textured paints and thick lead pencils made in France. They cost the kind of money that would instantly make my parentals go all tense and talk about things like prioritising and budgeting. DIY Corner was the royalty of craft supplies.

After a quick look for cameras, I looped my arm in Libby's and directed her over to the scrapbooking station.

"Here's the thing, this is the only section secluded enough. You'll need to come back here before you hide whatever you have, okay?" I whispered.

She gave me a mock salute and disappeared towards the paint section. I went to follow her when I noticed the elderly sales lady watching us with a small frown, causing the creases on her forehead to deepen. It was pretty easy to tell that she was suspicious of us; we were two teenagers in a store filled with tiny objects that could easily be taken.

I panicked slightly when her eyes locked with mine. There was no time to think and no chance to leave without seeming suspicious. It took a split second to make my decision and before any more time could pass, I smiled brightly at the woman and made my way over to the counter.

"Hello, ma'am, do you have a spare minute?" I asked her as innocently as I was capable of in the situation. "I could really use your opinion on something."

Her expression seemed to shift into sales assistant mode— authoritative but friendly. "Of course dear. How can I help?"

I directed her towards the aisle packed with black covered sketching pads and charcoals, but more importantly, furthest from Libby. I softly asked her what charcoal would be best to use in the sketch I was making for my mother's birthday. A little lie was the only way to keep the lady away from Libby.

"Your best option is to go with a thicker piece for your first draft," she said, handing me a heavy black stick of charcoal. "That way shading can be done a lot faster."

I thanked her with a smile and watched her wave to a man who had just walked through the entrance.

"I'm just going to see if that gentleman needs a hand with anything. If you need any more help just call out, sweetie."

She disappeared around the end of the aisle, and with a long exhale I gently placed the charcoal back where it belonged.

That was too close for my liking.

My fingers shook from the adrenaline and I couldn't calm myself down. Even though she left me alone, I wasn't going to stick around for her to return. I headed towards the exit before the lady could make her way to the counter. As I left the store, I motioned to Libby that time was up and that I would be in the food court.

* * *

"What happened to you? I turned around and you were gone. Did you chicken out?" Libby said. We took a seat in the middle of the crowded food court.

"The sales lady saw us. I kept her busy while you enjoyed yourself. You're welcome by the way." I sighed and tried to relax my shoulders. They were still tense from the encounter and I didn't want to end up with a sore back.

Unfortunately, there wasn't much I could do to stop the tremors that crawled under my skin and found their way to my hands. I looked like a smoker going through some crazy withdrawals. I really hoped no one was paying us any attention.

"So tell me, how did you do this time?" I asked, trying to sound as casual as possible under the circumstances.

With a wide smile, Libby placed her bag on the table. She didn't pull anything out. Instead she lightly stroked the bag with a mischievous grin on her face.

"Well, I got a lovely paintbrush set and seven different coloured paints," she said smugly. "Oh, I also got you a set."

"You got me something?" I stared at Libby with a bright smile. Just when you thought she was being predictable, she'd do something that would completely surprise you.

"Don't act so shocked. I figured you were preoccupied so I thought I'd pick up the slack." She shrugged. "Besides, what are friends for?"

"Aw, corny, but incredibly sweet. Thank you!"

"Shut up," she replied, shaking her hands out. "I'm hungry."

Libby stood up and walked leisurely over to the Chinese eatery to place her order. She didn't say anything; she just stood there with a blank, almost bored expression on her face. There wasn't even a slight quiver in her at all.

I joined her to buy my own lunch before returning to our table. The whole adventure had lasted about an hour, but it felt like we'd been at the mall for days. Now the adrenaline rush was starting to fade, I didn't feel like I'd changed at all. I was still the same old Nic; I hadn't turned into a hardened criminal—not as far as I could tell.

Maybe nothing was supposed to change. I slowly chewed on my food as I contemplated what had happened. What we did felt like a mixture of fun and something I had never felt before—danger.

"So what's the verdict?" Libby asked through a mouthful of fried rice. I cringed at her and waited until she had swallowed.

"It was fun, but only a one time deal," I said. "I've proved my point and that's all I wanted."

After I'd finished eating, I picked up my plastic plate and dropped it haphazardly in the rubbish. I had already called my mother to ask her to pick us up after we ate, so we headed out the front entrance to wait for our ride home.

"Hello, girls," Mum said when she pulled up twenty minutes later.

"Hey, Susan," Libby called out as she climbed into the back seat. There was no need for formalities since Libby was practically family. Actually, I figured my parents should've just adopted her considering she spent so much time at our house anyway. Libby's parents wanted to move her to a new school after they brought a massive property in Bellvale, but there was no way we were going to do that. Moving Libby into our spare room was the only way we could graduate together. She cried every night for the first week until the homesickness faded and our home became hers.

"Did you girls have fun?"

I looked at Libby through the side mirror and saw her wink at me. "Yeah, it was definitely an interesting trip." I smiled to myself as she and my mother started talking about the latest celebrity divorce.

I had no regrets over what happened, but I was done. I had gotten what I wanted from the adventure. Aiden was wrong about me and that's what really mattered. Now, all I wanted to do was focus on what was most important: sending my application to Murdoch and getting the hell out of this town.

3

The Master Thief and the Mastermind

Exactly two days, six hours and twenty-five minutes had passed since Libby and I went on our adventure, not that I was counting or anything. We hadn't talked about it since we arrived home that afternoon. However, I could tell Libby was itching to bring it up. Over the past two days she would flash her new make-up at me and wink whenever she could. When I saw her toying with her mosaic necklace in the hall between classes, and saying to one of the girls from her drama class "You'll never guess where I got it!", I finally snapped.

Muttering something like, "Can I talk to you for a minute?" I grabbed her arm and physically dragged her around the corner.

"Would you stop that already?!"

"Geez, someone is moody," she retorted. "What's up your arse?"

"You keep flaunting that stuff!" I hissed. "It's stolen property! You really want everyone to find out we committed a crime?"

"You're just a spoilsport." She crossed her arms and lifted her eyebrow. "If we were going to get caught, we would have by now. So take a chill pill."

She had a point. I didn't expect the police would launch some big investigation over a couple of stolen necklaces and some make-up. But it still made me grind my teeth that she was being so careless about keeping our secret.

"Okay, but just cool it a bit, will you?"

Libby rolled her eyes, but didn't argue. The bell rang and she quickly hugged me and told me she would meet me after class to go back to mine. It had become a tradition of ours to have a movie session every Friday night.

She disappeared in the crowd of people as they went to their classes. I made my way over to my English class and sat down in my assigned seat, trying my best to ignore Aiden's smug glances from across the room. As the teacher began discussing what Shakespeare's message was in Macbeth, I thought about just how wrong Aiden was about me. I might not have been kissed yet, but you couldn't say I'd gone through my whole life without a thrill.

∗ ∗ ∗

Half an hour through watching *Paranormal Activity* that evening, Libby turned to me. "Don't make any plans for tomorrow, Sunshine. We're going burning."

I tore my eyes from the screen and scrunched my face in confusion. "What?"

"You know, stealing," she said, as if it was the most obvious thing on the planet. "I know you said it was a one-time deal …"

"It was a one-time deal," I confirmed. "Wait, why are you calling it burning?"

She picked herself up from the floor and reached for her drink. "Well, we're going to need a code word. We can't just say we're going stealing every time, can we, genius? In case a teacher hears or something."

I gave her an incredulous look. *Every time*? This wasn't going to become a habit. Sometimes I really had no idea what went on in her head, but I knew better than to argue with her.

"I guess that makes sense, but why burning?"

Libby placed her drink back on the table and leant against her pillow, settling back into her makeshift bed.

"Because it's badass, obviously." She stretched her feet out and snuggled back under the covers. "People will think we're up to something real kinky."

"You're disgusting."

"I'm just better adapted to the criminal life than you are."

That's what we were now, wasn't it? Criminals. I sighed and settled back down to watch the film, but Libby wasn't finished trying to persuade me.

"We could try something different, you know." When I didn't reply, she turned her head away from the screen and looked at me. "I know you didn't really enjoy it as much as you thought you would." She shrugged. "Maybe it just wasn't much of a challenge for you."

"What do you mean?"

She grabbed a fistful of popcorn and pushed the bowl towards me. I took a handful and started chewing one piece at a time. Anything to distract myself from really giving what Libby had to say a proper thought.

"You're a thinker, Nic. You need something that's going to be a little more difficult," she said through a mouthful of popcorn. "I'm not saying that you are bad at the actual theft part, but you're more of the mastermind."

"Mastermind?" I frowned. This was the second time Libby had used that term. I wasn't sure where she was going with it because, honestly, I never knew where Libby's mind would go.

"Yeah, bloody genius isn't it?" Her eyes lit up and a grin broke across her face. "I figured since we're the freaking wonder twins, we needed nicknames. Your mutant brain makes you the mastermind and I'm the master thief."

I laughed so hard that I felt a cramp forming under my ribcage. I didn't mind it though, at least not always. Sometimes it would be nice if she could be serious, but I guess after panicking during the last few days that someone would find out what we did, it was nice to be able to laugh again.

"You're such a dork."

"Says the one who practically hibernates in the library." She threw a piece of popcorn at me and laughed.

I nibbled on a half-popped kernel as I contemplated what Libby had said. Sure, it was tempting; I wasn't going to lie about that. There was something addictive about taking whatever you wanted, and Libby was right: my inner nerd enjoyed the mental challenge. However, this was only supposed to be a one-time thing. Aiden's sly words kept coming back to mind. Maybe the first adventure was to prove him wrong, but this time I needed to do something to prove myself wrong. I needed to know that I was capable of whatever I put my mind to. I needed to feel that spark. Quite simply, I wanted to be bad again.

"So, what do you have in mind?" I sighed.

Libby smiled smugly and tapped the stack of DVDs near her foot. "When was the last time your parents gave you any money for DVDs? Don't you think it's time we updated your collection?"

4
Stepping it up

The smell of buttery popcorn from the night before was still in the air when I entered the lounge. I sat down and picked up the DVD carry case that we were planning to use, making sure it was small enough to hide.

"What are you doing up so early?" I spun around hastily when I heard my mother's voice.

She was dressed in a form fitting pencil skirt and a white business blouse that hugged her curves flawlessly. She usually only wore that outfit when she was going to see the bank manager or another financial planner. She walked over to the kitchen and switched on the coffee machine. I followed her and sat down at the table as she began to make breakfast.

Before I could answer her, Dad swept through the door with the morning newspaper in hand.

"Hey squirt, you're up early," he said.

I looked at him and frowned. He was also dressed as if he was off to a business meeting. The black pants and light blue dress shirt that he wore still had the crease marks that new clothing always had.

"Why are you both so dressed up?" I asked, although I had already guessed.

"Your father and I are going to the bank." Mum sat down and gave me a forced smile. "We're going to see if we can take out a loan against our mortgage."

I nodded as I bit down on some toast and chewed slowly. Another loan.

Mum continued to rattle off their plans for the day, but after the mention of the bank I couldn't focus on anything else. I knew money was tight lately, but I didn't think it was tight to the point that my parents needed to borrow money again. The toast in my mouth tasted more like dry cardboard when I realised that I was partially guilty. My parents always complained about the extra money I would ask for to spend on shopping trips with Libs, but I had never thought that maybe they couldn't actually afford it. I certainly never gave them much thought when I talked about moving to Los Angeles for university, which wasn't going to be cheap. If there was an award for the worst daughter of the year, I'm sure I would have been the number one choice.

Libby stumbled into the kitchen, taking a seat next to me and rubbing the sleep from her eyes.

"Morning, Susan," she yawned. "Morning, Mr Edwards."

"Good morning, sweetie," Mum replied. "Late night?"

"Yep, you know what Nic and I are like," she said, tucking into a bowl of cornflakes that Dad had slipped in front of her.

"Let me guess," Dad said, placing his hand on his forehead and pretending to be in deep thought. "You girls stayed up until the early hours watching horror movies?"

"Are we really that predictable?"

"Of course not, honey." Mum looked at Dad knowingly and winked.

My parents could be such dorks. I smiled and tossed a piece of toast at Libby, who was humming softly while she ate.

"So, what are you girls getting up to today?" Dad asked absentmindedly, flipping through his paper to the sports section.

"Oh, nothing too exciting," Libby answered before I could swallow my mouthful of juice. "Just burning."

I almost spat my drink all over the kitchen bench. Choking

slightly, I tried to control my breathing while glaring at Libby. Was she crazy? She had to be certifiably insane to even consider using the stupid code word in front of my parents. Mum start rubbing circles on my back when I fell into a coughing fit.

"You okay, Nicky?"

"Yeah m'fine," I answered once my airways were clear. "Just went down the wrong way."

Sitting back down, I kicked Libby under the table. She turned to face me with a bright smile and laughter in her eyes, having way too much fun at my expense.

"What do you mean by burning?" Dad asked once we had settled down.

"Oh, it's just slang," I said, trying to control my steadily rising heartbeat. I was going to get Libby back for this, like changing the password to her Facebook account before we left. "It means shopping. We heard it on some English show and now everyone's saying it."

Relief flooded back through my body when my parents changed their focus to discussing how long it would take to get to the bank with the traffic delays blocking the highway. When I knew they weren't going to notice, I smacked Libby on the arm with a level of force that I wouldn't feel guilty about. Although, let's face it, she deserved much worse.

"What?" she whispered. "I knew you'd cover me."

"Not the point," I snapped. "We don't need to draw any unnecessary attention."

"Okay, okay, I'm sorry," she said with a smirk that told me she wasn't sorry at all.

I hastily kissed my parents on the forehead when Libby signalled that she was ready and told them that we were catching the bus to the Bellvale Mall. We grabbed our bags and headed to the bus stop down the street from my home. As we waited, Libby pulled out a small compact mirror to check her makeup while I nervously twirled a piece of my hair through my fingers.

"Don't be such a baby, we've got this." She placed her compact mirror back into her pocket and grabbed the hand that was tangled in my hair.

"I know, okay?" I replied harshly, flagging our bus with a wave of my hand.

I pushed myself away from her and climbed onto the bus, claiming the back seat. The engine started with a roar and the bus pulled away from the stop. I settled back into my chair and tried to relax my body. I wanted to do this, I knew that, and nothing was going to change.

"So, this is it?" Libby sprawled out on the backseat and rolled her shoulders.

"This is it."

Fifteen minutes later, the bus pulled up with a jolt at the front of the mall. I wasn't sure why but I felt like a death row prisoner on the way to my execution. I silently rose from my seat and wrapped my bag around my shoulder. Libby stretched her back until she heard a satisfying pop and then pushed her way to the front of the bus. How she was able to be so calm still amazed me. As we thanked the driver and made our way towards the centre, we talked quietly through the plans we had made the night before, trying to smooth out any loopholes.

"So, we're all sorted?" Libby asked, popping a piece of gum in her mouth. "Last chance to be a chicken."

"Yep, this is it," I repeated, ignoring her comment. "Unless you don't think your head is in it?"

"Do you even have to ask? Obviously I'm committed." Sure, she sounded convinced, but her face cracked enough for me to really take notice. Finally, I was able to see something else besides confidence. She looked drained of any emotion other than self-assurance. Now, I could tell she wasn't as excited as she had been the first time we did this.

It was good to know I wasn't the only one feeling a little hesitant.

"Okay then, let's go shall we?"

She nodded and began to walk towards the front entrance, only to be sidetracked by an obnoxiously loud wolf whistle.

Great. Another damn thing to worry about.

"Oh look, it's your boyfriend," Libby snickered, blowing a kiss to the two boys out front.

I looked over and saw Aiden standing beside the front entrance with one of the boys we'd seen him with before. The sandy blonde boy wore a light blue uniform and was slowly devouring a pizza. Aiden bumped fists with the other boy, wetting his lips and winking at me.

"Well, if it isn't my favourite girl and my favourite flirt."

"Naw, Aiden, it's always a pleasure to see you in that tight, tight jacket of yours," Libby practically purred. She extended her hand for him to kiss and he returned his gaze to me.

"Come on, Edwards. Let's see that smile of yours." He brushed his hand across my face. The heat from his palm was like a branding iron to my cheek. I slapped his hand away and stepped back, grabbing Libby's arm in a tight grip. I didn't want to spend any longer around Aiden than was absolutely necessary.

"I'm afraid we ought to go." My level of sarcasm couldn't get any higher. "We really should do this again sometime, you know, in the far, far future."

I pulled Libby away before Aiden could reply and darted through the door. "What was that?" I snapped at her.

"What?" she said defensively. "I was just being friendly."

"Why do you encourage him?" I let go of her hand and walked briskly towards our chosen target, the department store, Wild Thing.

"Don't be like that, Sunshine," she said soothingly. "He's just trying to give you the hot beef injection."

Gross! I scrunched my face in disgust and rubbed harshly at my forehead. I didn't know why he got under my skin so much, but Libby certainly didn't help by egging him on. There was a reminder of him almost everywhere I went. Even his vanilla scent seemed to cling to my clothes whenever he was around.

"Wait a minute." Libby came to an abrupt halt. "You totally want to tap that, don't you?"

"Of course not, that's ridiculous."

"Bullshit, that's why he gets to you so much."

I saw the entrance to Wild Thing and picked up my pace. The department store was one of the biggest in Australia and had a section for everything. It also had a lot of customers, meaning a lot of distraction and not enough staff. According to my "mastermind" plan, this was the perfect place to hit. In record time I reached the front entrance, which was drowning with posters promoting their latest discounted items. The brightly lit store was packed with people and the air was filled with chatter and registers beeping as items were scanned in.

"Hey, don't ignore me." Libby managed to catch up to me and tapped me lightly on the shoulder.

"I'm not ignoring you," I said calmly. "Can we just focus on what we came here for?"

She huffed dramatically, before taking a steady breath. "All right, but we'll be talking about this later."

I walked through the store, trying to control my breathing. When I saw the sign for the DVD section, I felt a hand tighten round my heart. One part of me never wanted to do anything remotely close to theft again. Last weekend had been so terrifying that I still felt sick whenever I thought about it. I could already hear the disappointment in my parents' voices if they ever found out.

The other part of me, a part I had never felt before, finally awoke and filled with excitement. I loved how my heart sped up and adrenaline flooded through my body. This had become more than just proving Aiden wrong; it was a chance for me to finally feel alive in a town where everyone seemed paralysed in the ordinary. My skin crawling with electricity, I followed the sign towards our target.

Although the department wasn't massive, it did have four decent sized aisles fully stocked with movies from the past five decades. Each section had a glossy sign above it displaying the genre. I crept over to the Action aisle and gingerly flicked through the movies. I had absolutely no idea what I was looking for. Despite all the planning, we hadn't thought about what we were actually going to take, because after all, it wasn't really about the movies. I flipped through a few more DVDs absent-mindedly until a dark silhouette of a man caught my eye. A chuckle bubbled up my throat when I saw that the movie was *Mission Impossible.*

Now that's irony for you.

I picked the DVD out and made my way over to Libby. She had a stack of DVDs in one hand and was browsing with the other. I took one look at her collection and laughed quietly. She had picked up every movie she could find that had some kind of connection with theft, even *Ocean's Eleven!*

"You're not very subtle."

"Please," she shrugged. "How could I not?"

I smiled at her and shook my head. I don't even think she understood what we were doing or how serious it could be.

"Come on, let's finish this so we can head home."

We discreetly walked closer to the bathroom, the only part of the store without security cameras. We had planned this out the night before—well, I had planned, and Libby had said things like "Sure, whatever, Sunshine", while she checked out the cute guys in the movie.

Inside our bags we had packed an empty DVD wallet and

a nail file to slice through the plastic wrappers. All we had to do was slip the DVDs out of their cases into the wallet, and chuck the cases—complete with security tags—into the bathroom bin.

Piece of cake.

Just as we emerged from the aisles and were about to pass the lay-by desk, a slightly chubby man cut us off and started talking to the lay-by lady. He wore a loose fitting white business shirt that had the word SECURITY sewn into the back of it in large bold letters.

There was no mistaking who he was. They hadn't noticed us yet, but our pathway was blocked. No way were we going to be able to sneak past them to get to the bathroom.

"Crap," Libby whispered frantically. "Crap, crap, crap, crap!"

"Calm down, will you?" I said, gripping her shoulder.

"Oh, all right, Ghandi, what are we going to do now? We can't exactly walk past them with a handful of DVDs."

I had to think fast. We could wait for him to leave and for the lady to turn away from the desk, but that would mean breaking our "quick in, quick out" rule. Waiting was definitely not an option.

We could drop the DVDs and leave it for another day, except we were already in the store and there was no way I was going to go through all that again. We couldn't wait and couldn't leave, that meant one thing.

"Distraction," I said out loud.

"Excuse me?"

"We need to distract both of them so that we can slip you in without being noticed."

"Oh, that's just brilliant. How do you suggest we do that?"

"Well, there's one thing we can do."

I had a few ideas about what we'd have to do if we were ever in need of a distraction but I hadn't given them too much thought. I didn't really see us needing to distract someone in any other way than by simply asking a question.

"Wait, do you want me to start messing up the kids' section or something?" Libby asked with a mischievous glint in her eyes.

"What? No," I scoffed. "What is it with you and destroying things?"

She smirked and tilted her head slightly, waiting for me to continue.

We'd need to direct their attention away from the bathroom, not cause a massive scene.

It was basically like playing Russian roulette. The security guard was the gun and one false move would mean it was all over for us. I knew it was going to take trust and one hell of a lie to get to the bathroom undetected. Once, I was late to class because I had slept through my alarm and missed the morning assembly where the roll was marked. I couldn't risk ruining my perfect attendance so I convinced my teacher I had been there all along. It took tears and a frantic high pitch voice for him to believe me, so I knew what I needed to do now.

Thankful once again that I took drama as an elective, I inhaled and focused on channelling enough sadness to start the tears. Having been on edge all day, my emotions were already raw enough; it only took a few seconds before I felt the familiar burning in my eyes. Libby watched me with a confused frown when the tears started to form, but she collected herself quickly enough to weave through the aisles until she was perched across from the lay-by desk. Taking a minute to pretend I was browsing through the DVDs, I picked up the first two that my eyes fell upon and pulled my facial features closer together so it appeared as if I was barely holding it together. I made a mental note to give my drama teacher a present for focusing so much on the dramatic side of acting. With the security guard right ahead of me, my nerves rose until there was an uncomfortable weight in the pit of my stomach. I only hesitated for a second before my harder side took over.

Any and all doubt I had was long gone.

With a deep breath, I paced over to where the sales assistant and security guard were continuing their conversation. I glanced at Libby at the last second, only to see her slipping out of the aisle and ducking towards the bathroom. As my drama teacher always said, it was time to shine, darling.

"Excuse me, I'm so sorry to bother you." I took all the nerves and fear that I had before and pushed them to the surface, making sure the tears slipped down my cheeks.

"Don't be sorry, dear. Is everything okay?" The sales assistant patted my arm lightly. She had soft green eyes that were so round and kind they made the lady look a little like Bambi. Her red hair was a few shades lighter than mine and layered with chunky blonde highlights. "Stay here sweetheart, I'll grab you a chair."

She looked up at the security guard and gestured for him to stay with me while she went to the backroom. I gave him a watery smile and sniffed quietly. His face was pulled into a stern expression, but his eyes were soft and staring down at me in concern. The sales assistant, whose badge said her name was Tahlia, came back with a chair and waited for me to talk. I swiped my sleeve across my nose and quickly launched into the story I had seen in some trashy teen drama. I cried as I told them that I had spent the entire day without any luck trying to find the perfect gift for my brother's birthday, hoping whatever I did find would cheer him up. He had been depressed ever since he saw his doctor and found out that he had a brain tumour.

I don't know how I felt about telling such a terrible story or why I chose it considering I didn't even have a brother, but

I knew the security guard wouldn't be able to handle a girl in tears. Barely five minutes had passed and already I could tell that he and Tahlia believed my story. I mean, why wouldn't they? To them, I had no reason to lie.

Tahlia squeezed my shoulder gently and gave me a gap-toothed smile.

I felt bad lying to her. She was so kind and caring to me while I sat there and took advantage of her. Guilt started to surface and I felt a real tear start to mix with the fake ones. This wasn't the person I wanted to be. I didn't take advantage of nice people for something as stupid as stealing DVDs I'd probably never watch. It was decided then; I wasn't going to do this again, no matter what Libby said.

"Look, I'm sorry, I really just need to use the bathroom and wash my face," I said after taking a few seconds to relax my body. "Would it be okay if I left these with you for a few minutes?"

I pointed to the decoy DVDs that I had tucked securely under my arm. No matter how I felt now, I still had one last job to finish.

"Of course you can, dear. They'll be right here when you come back," Tahlia said with a bright smile. "Now cheer up, your brother is going to love whatever you get him."

She patted my knee and then took the DVDs from my hands. I smiled at the security guard who gave me a quick wink and swiftly walked towards the baby department.

With the man gone and Tahlia moving further down the desk, I ducked into the bathroom and knocked twice on the end stall.

"Took you long enough," Libby muttered as she continued to peel the DVDs out of their cases and shove them into the carry case we brought along. "Did she go for it?"

"Course she did," I snapped. I still felt guilty over the whole thing. "I told you it would work. Now let's get this done already."

We continued to silently rip the remaining DVDs from their packaging and slide them into the carry case. Neither of us said anything, and soon enough Libby was jamming the case into her bag and burying it under her purse while I discarded the packaging in the nearby hygiene bin.

"How are we with time?" I asked.

"Well, we're not late, that's for sure." Libby checked her watch and pulled her bag onto her back. "We're at seven minutes all up."

"Smart ass," I said as I slid open the lock to the cubicle.

"You wound me," she mocked. "I'm not one to waste time when we're burning and I suppose a little part of me was worried someone was going to walk in. And I mean a minuscule part."

I stared at her as she exhaled slowly. Her fingers drummed on the bag where the case of stolen DVDs was stashed, and there was a tiny sheen of sweat on her upper lip. She shot me a sharp look, as if forbidding me to notice that this was stressing her out too.

"Let's just get out of here before the assistant comes looking for me," I said, swinging the door open and walking out of the stall. "I did act pretty distraught so I wouldn't put it past her to check on me."

I came to a complete halt when I caught a reflection in the mirror that wasn't mine. My heart started to pound so hard it was all I could hear. I turned to face the mystery person. There was no way they hadn't at least partially heard what we were talking about. My mouth gaped in surprise when I saw a familiar black leather jacket and powerful smirk.

"Afternoon, ladies," Aiden said as he placed an arm on top of the paper towel dispenser and narrowed his eyes in amusement. "My, we have been busy."

5

The Proposal

He leant against the dispenser with a confident smile and an amused glint in his eyes. I couldn't bring myself to look at Libby in case the fear I was feeling was mirrored on her face. If carefree Libby was scared then we really were screwed.

"What the hell are you doing in the ladies' toilets, Aiden?" Libby finally broke the silence that had fallen between us. There was a little shake in her voice that hadn't been there before.

"Well, I loved what I saw so much that I just had to come in here and congratulate you," he crooned. He kept his eyes trained on me the whole time, which really started to freak me out.

"I have no idea what you're talking about," Libby snapped.

Okay, I didn't like this Libby at all. Her hands shook slightly at her sides, which only made me feel uneasy. She was the one who was supposed to tell me to grow a pair and suck it up, not act like we had just been caught cheating on our English final. Although, this situation would definitely rank higher on the "how screwed are you" scale.

"Come off it," Aiden said with an air of smugness. "Greg works the security desk so I had front row tickets to your little show."

"Who?"

"You know the tall guy I was with this morning?" he asked.

"Oh yeah," she said casually, and just like that she was back in friend mode with Aiden. They were having a perfectly normal catch-up in the ladies' toilets of a store we had just stolen from. Only Libby—no, only Libby and Aiden—could possibly think this was an appropriate time and place for a bit of chatting and flirting.

The conversation filtered out and I was tempted to walk out of the bathroom and avoid the entire situation. Aiden chose that moment to look up and meet my gaze. I needed to think of something to get out of there and I needed to do it quickly.

"Aiden, it's not what it looks like."

I cringed. Of course I'd say the lamest sentence imaginable. He knew exactly what we had done and judging by the smirk on his face, he was aware that I knew.

"Oh isn't it, Edwards?" He crossed his arms and turned to face me. "So you didn't take some DVDs from the rack, give fake ones to the sales assistant while telling her a lie about your supposed brother, before meeting your partner-in-crime in here so you could slip the real DVDs into your bag?"

All I could do was look at him blankly, opening and closing my mouth like a cartoon character. I had no idea what to do or say. For someone who had a brain like Scofield, I wasn't doing too well.

"Okay, so it's exactly what it looks like." Libby pulled her arms tightly across her chest. "What are you waiting for? I bet you can't wait to see the security guy cop a feel."

My head spun to face her so fast that I was sure my neck would have snapped right off if it were physically possible. Libby had voiced what we were both thinking and I literally felt sick. Sick enough that if I didn't get out of there soon, we were going to need a cleaner.

Confusion filtered across Aiden's face briefly before his confident smirk returned. He'd had such a sweet smile back when we were friends, but now Aiden smirked so often that he probably couldn't change it back.

His eyes locked with mine and I saw something different in them. They were soft and full of sincerity, almost like when we were younger. His gaze was fixated on me so intently that heat rose up my neck and I quickly lowered my eyes to the floor, breaking our contact.

He pushed himself off the dispenser and walked closer to us. I could feel the body heat radiating from him and his usual vanilla scent was starting to make me feel a little drunk. The type of drunk where everything seemed more intense than usual.

"I wasn't planning on turning you two in," he said sincerely. "Like I said before, I wanted to congratulate you. I haven't seen anyone with guts like you two since, well, me. I guess I better pick up my game then, huh?"

I don't know what the hell Aiden was playing at but he certainly never gave up an opportunity to sell me out.

Aiden turned to leave, grabbing onto the door handle. He paused and looked over his shoulder back at us. "You coming or what?" he said.

I stood frozen in place, unable to comprehend what had just happened. It had to be a trap. It was the only thing that really made sense. At least the only thing I could think of.

I focused on Libby as she moved towards the door. "Where are you going?"

"Where do you think?" she said, turning to face me. "I'm going to find out why Aiden just saved our butts."

When I didn't reply, she sighed softly and placed her hands on my shoulders.

"Don't you want to know why he's keeping our secret?" she said, staring directly at me. "Come on, Sunshine, it'll only take a minute." Her tone was soft, nervous.

I rubbed my forehead as I felt my resolve weaken. I could barely hide the fact that I was just as desperate as Libby to know what the real situation was. Aiden wasn't dobbing us in and I had to know what his angle was, even if it meant that I'd be doing exactly what he wanted by following him.

With my eyes closed, I breathed in as much as I could before exhaling and gesturing towards the door in defeat. "Even though I'm agreeing to this, I just want you to know that I think this is a terrible idea."

"Noted."

She grabbed my hand and pulled me out of the bathroom and past the empty lay-by desk. I couldn't see Tahlia or the security guard anywhere nearby, which was a relief. I don't think I'd be able to explain why I was rushing out of the bathroom with another person when I went in there alone and in tears. Libby kept walking like there was some kind of sale she couldn't wait to get to. I trailed behind her for a little longer until we caught a glimpse of a familiar leather jacket.

We followed Aiden to the food court where I dropped myself at the first empty table I could find and waited for the other two to buy lunch. Libby returned with a salad sandwich and we stayed silent until Aiden joined us a few minutes later, sitting across from me. It felt a little too normal for us three to be having lunch together. This little role-play we had going was seriously getting old.

"So what's going on, Aiden?"

"Straight to the point I see. You don't waste time, do you?"

I gave him a pointed look and pulled my lips into a tight line. "Not when it comes to you."

What the hell was that? I snapped my mouth shut the moment I realised what I had said. It wasn't supposed to come out like that. I was trying to think of an insult, but my brain was on empty. I lowered my eyes and frowned at my own weirdness. When did I decide to just hand Aiden the chance to get the upper hand on me?

"Is that so?" Aiden spoke so softly I almost missed it.

I lifted my eyes from the table and caught him staring right at me. Clearly I wasn't the only one acting like a personality transplant patient. Aiden had the perfect opening to ridicule me and he didn't go for it. He could have laughed right in my face, but instead he continued to hold my gaze until I could clearly make out the emotions flashing across his eyes. They still came across as dark and cold, there was no denying that, except now they softened around the edges.

"Are you going to tell us what you wanted us to come for," Libby arched her eyebrow in amusement, "or are you going to keep eye-banging Nic here?"

I broke our eye contact at the mention of my name. There was no way I was going to look at Libby when I couldn't stop the pink flush forming across my cheeks from embarrassment. Aiden shifted from his soft smile back to his infamous smirk, almost as if the softness had never been there at all.

"Well, I have a proposal for you ladies." He leant forward in his seat and clasped his hands together on the table like he was conducting an interview.

"A proposal?" I asked.

"That's correct."

"Are we talking about a sexy proposal?" Libby crossed her legs and leant against the table. Sometimes I wondered if she had an off switch when it came to snark. Once I asked her mum whether she had always been like that and she said that when Libby was born, she gave the doctor a wink and the middle finger. Her answer was confirmation enough. Clearly Libby took after her mum.

Aiden's smirk grew deeper as he pulled himself forward to mirror Libby. "Not this time, gorgeous. A group of us are planning a massive heist," he said in just above a whisper. "It's nothing too serious, just a bunch of us hitting up a few chain stores for their clothes and whatever else."

Well, that was definitely the last thing I ever expected Aiden to say. If I weren't so surprised, I would have laughed. I had never seen this side of Aiden before, and frankly I didn't know what to make of it. DVDs and make-up were one thing, but a chain store heist was a little too *Ocean's Eleven* for my liking. This was absolutely crazy and I was crazy for still sitting there when it was obvious this was only going to end badly.

"A group of you?" Libby broke the awkward silence that had fallen around us.

"Yeah. There's five of us including me," he replied. "Seven, if you ladies join us."

"Chain stores, huh?" I whipped my head around and stared at Libby with a mixture of shock and disbelief. I couldn't believe she was even considering this, especially after we almost got caught by security earlier. If that wasn't a warning against stealing then I had no clue what was.

"Yeah, we're going to split into two groups and take on two different places." Aiden looked between us with a determined spark in his eye. "And then we're going to meet up back at a safe location and go from there."

"Oh yeah, because that's a great idea, said nobody ever," I snapped.

This was all sounding so ridiculous. I frowned at both of them as I wrapped my arms tightly around myself.

"Ignore her," Libby said, giving me a pointed look. "Sunshine has a habit of giving Oscar-worthy reactions."

I'll give her a reaction all right.

"I think it's cute actually," Aiden cut in before I could retaliate. "Besides, you will both get a cut of whatever we sell the stuff for. I'm sure you'll put the money to good use."

I clamped my mouth shut and shifted my eyes in his direction. Did he think I had been stealing DVDs because I didn't have the money to buy them? He smiled slightly, showing a few of his smooth white teeth. Conversation dropped and we sat there in silence for a few moments, picking at our lunch. This entire situation seemed so surreal that it felt like we were in a trashy remake of the *Godfather* and Aiden was making us an offer we couldn't refuse.

I couldn't cope with it any longer, sitting there as if being asked to take part in a heist was the kind of normal thing that happened to me at lunchtime. I pushed my tray back.

"I'm going to the toilet," I announced.

"You just came out of the toilet," Aiden said, raising a teasing eyebrow.

"Yes, but I wasn't, I mean, I didn't …"

Great, so now I was discussing bodily functions with a boy who never seemed to have a problem finding excuses to laugh at me. Real smooth.

I got halfway to the toilets, my brain spinning out of control, when suddenly I had to stop. What if this was a joke? It wouldn't exactly be out of character for Aiden to wind us up like this. I could just imagine him telling his friends later, "… and she thought it was for *real!*" They would wet themselves, thinking about how I gave some prissy moral speech about this imaginary robbery. If it was real, why on earth would he ask me and Libby anyway?

I marched back to the table. "Why?" I asked, breaking in on their conversation.

"Excuse me?"

"Why do you want our help?"

Aiden looked at me as if I had gone mad, but that was better than his perma-smirk. He straightened his back and pulled his chair closer to the table.

"You really don't know?" He stared in disbelief. "Edwards, you're the best thinker out there. You think I've forgotten the senior prank already?"

Libby giggled. As usual, that had been something she talked me into organising, but I was the one who came up with the idea of putting detergent in the junior class's instruments before their annual concert. Bubbles everywhere.

"We never did get caught for that!" Libby said.

"Of course not," Aiden replied. "It was well planned. And then there's you with your freakishly fast fingers." She blew him a kiss with them to confirm it. "I would have thought it was obvious why I wanted you both to join us."

Without a word, I turned and headed for the bathroom again.

Alone in the cubicle, I finally had the chance to think about it. Aiden was serious. At least, I thought so. So why wasn't I telling him to shove it? Obvious, really: because of the money. I mean, we had done pretty well so far and this new adventure would solve my money problems. My parents were probably still at the bank, arranging a loan as I sat there. If this went right, I could make a dent in the tuition for Murdoch, even if it was only a little one. It would be enough to cover me until I could find a decent job and pay for the rest. This was a chance to have the future I wanted without bankrupting my parents.

It was also a chance to end up in jail for much longer than the four years of university.

I stared at the adverts on the cubicle door and tried to calm the butterflies that were raging a war inside my stomach. Actually, screw the butterflies; I had full grown magpies swooping around. It was such a huge risk—but no risk, no reward, right?

I slowly exhaled, and came to a decision. As much as I wanted to reject Aiden's offer, I knew I couldn't. But that didn't mean I was going to let the others know.

I returned to the table and took a moment to stare the other two down like they did in those old western films. I needed to play this right. As long as they didn't know I had a bigger stake in this than they thought, I could still have some control over the heist. If I left Libby and Aiden with all the control then we might as well call the police ourselves and invite them to join us.

Libby opened her mouth just as I held up a finger to silence her. I knew exactly what she was going to say. She'd tell me how this would be a perfect way to make some money without having to flip burgers every weekend of our senior year and that I should stop being such a baby.

"Okay."

"Okay?" Aiden crinkled his forehead and narrowed his eyes like he was working on some ridiculously hard statistical equation. "What changed your mind?"

"That's not for you to know." I frowned. "All that matters is I'm agreeing to meet the others. I'll make my decision when I know what I'm working with."

I held Aiden's gaze while he appeared to have some sort of internal power struggle. Libby cleared her throat and stuck her hand out for Aiden to shake. He seemed a little dazed and gave me a look that suggested he was trying to analyse me. Libby wore that same expression whenever she attempted to do her maths homework.

Finally Aiden turned to Libby and shook her hand. When he held his hand out to me, his infamous smirk was back in place. "Now that we have that sorted, how are you ladies getting home?"

"We're taking the bus."

"No you're not," Aiden replied, standing up and throwing his rubbish in the bin across the table. "My car is out front. I'll drive you back. It'll give us a chance to talk more details."

We agreed to the lift and followed Aiden out to the car park. I knew he had gotten his licence earlier in the year, but I didn't know he already had a car. We continued to walk across a few more lanes until we stopped next to a sleek black Mitsubishi Lancer. He pressed the remote to unlock the doors and climbed into the driver's side. Libby quickly spread out across the back seat so I slipped into the passenger's side and secured my seat belt.

As we merged onto the highway back to Silverlake, I glanced at Libby through the side mirror. She gave me what should have been a reassuring wink, but I wasn't feeling it. The dynamic duo that we seemed to be was starting to feel a little less endearing and a lot more like a chokehold.

After a long, quiet drive, Aiden pulled up to my driveway and put the car in park.

"So we're meeting up at my house tomorrow night," he said, twisting in his seat and draping his arm over the back of my seat. "Everyone is getting there around midnight, so any time around then is fine."

I narrowed my eyes as I took in what he said. "Why midnight?" I asked. "Isn't that a bit late for a chain store heist? Nothing will be open."

Aiden dropped his gaze for a moment but quickly brought it back to look me straight in the eye. "Yeah it is," he confirmed. "But we're only drawing up plans tomorrow. The date of the actual heist is yet to be determined."

Libby unbuckled her seatbelt and pulled herself forward, holding onto my headrest for support. "So what will we be doing?"

"Well, since planning is her forte, I thought Edwards could help Noah put together the game plan. He talks like he's in an episode of *Mad Men,* but he's nice so you'll both love him," he replied with a quick flash of his flirtatious smile. "And I thought you could help Greg and Brooke with the actual theft part. They are our main thieves so you'll want to have a chat with them."

"Sounds like a plan to me," Libby replied cheerfully as she exited the car and walked over to Aiden's window. "I'll see you tomorrow night, handsome."

Libby sauntered towards the front door of my house as I unbuckled my own seatbelt. My hands were slightly shaky as the memories from today caught up to me. I guess I was more nervous about tomorrow than I thought. I kept imagining what would happen if we were caught and what kind of trouble we would face. Without much thought, I mumbled a quick good-bye to Aiden and started to open the door when a warm hand gripped lightly around my wrist.

"Wait."

The softness had returned to Aiden's eyes and he was staring at me so tenderly that I felt almost naked under his gaze. His eyes flicked down to my lips and I subconsciously licked them. His usual honey coloured irises seemed to grow darker as he leant slightly closer. My heart started to beat erratically as I realised what he was doing.

Aiden Campbell was going to kiss me.

My own eyes dropped to his mouth and I watched as his teeth chewed lightly on his bottom lip. He leant even closer and I started moving towards him, magnetically. I don't know what on earth I was doing. My brain kept shouting at me to stop before I wasted my first kiss on someone as arrogant as Aiden. Literally anyone else would have been a better option, but I couldn't stop myself from moving even closer.

Sometimes I really hated hormones and Aiden's incredibly intoxicating scent. We were so close I could feel his breath ghost across my lips and smell the hint of peppermint laced through it. We locked eyes again just as his nose grazed mine delicately, but instead of connecting our lips he pulled back suddenly.

"You know I'd never let anything or anyone hurt you, right?" he said a little breathlessly.

I wasn't sure whether he was talking about the heist or whether he was talking about himself. But now that there was space between us, I was finally able to regain control over myself. I pulled my bag up from the floor and opened the door. Before I left, I turned to face him.

"Promise?"

"Double promise," he replied, starting the engine.

I slid out of my seat and shut the door behind me. I gave a smile before Aiden pulled out of the driveway and out of sight. As soon as he was gone, I took a deep breath in and slowly exhaled through my nose.

What the hell was that almost kiss about and what did he mean by not letting anyone hurt me? And why did he pull away? More importantly, why did I care so much? Sure, he acted different when it was just the two of us alone. He almost seemed to melt into this soft and tender guy who could make you breathless without touching you. But he was still the boy who dropped me to impress his new friends and insulted me every time we saw each other. I had a moment of weakness, that's all.

It was never going to happen again.

I was keeping my first kiss for someone special and never once did I ever see Aiden fitting that description. Except, our bodies had been so close and in that moment I wanted nothing more than to bridge the gap between us. But, he was still Aiden—Sterling High hottie and grade A jerk. Whatever was suddenly going on with Aiden and me would have to stop ASAP.

I took one last deep breath and walked inside my house. One way or another, tomorrow was going to be an interesting day.

6
Surprises

Tick, tock, tick, tock. The only sound that filled the lounge room was the rhythmic ticking of the mosaic wall clock right across from the couch I was sitting on. It was late Sunday night, but we weren't game enough to leave for Sasha's until we knew for certain that my parents were asleep. Although they had said goodnight and left for bed half an hour earlier, we definitely didn't want to risk them coming downstairs and finding us missing. I wasn't exactly fond of the possibility of being grounded until retirement age if we were caught. So, we were going to wait an extra few minutes regardless of how desperate Libby was to get moving. She had been standing beside the clock since the moment my parents left, checking the time every five seconds and huffing in annoyance.

I tried to distract myself with the TV guide, flicking through the pages until I found an article on the latest Kardashian scandal. It was far from literary genius but I would much rather read that rubbish than torment myself by thinking about what would happen when we got to Sasha's.

I would've said that I was pumped but that would have been completely bogus. Honestly, I was a little nervous about meeting with Aiden and his group, especially after the incident in the car the day before. I still hadn't really worked out what the hell was going on there, and on top of that we were talking about stealing again. Maybe agreeing to this hadn't been such a good idea. I mean, the money would be amazing, but how many times could we go on these little adventures before we got caught?

My head started to throb as I attempted to pull my focus back to the article. It would have been much easier if Libby didn't insist on tapping impatiently against the clock's glass covering with her index finger.

"Stop that."

Libby sighed dramatically and joined me on the couch. Taking her away from her task was a sucky idea because now that she had no distractions, she turned to me with a smile that promised trouble.

"What?"

"Nothing."

I dropped my eyes back to the guide and attempted to ignore the feeling of her eyes boring into the side of my face.

"Okay seriously, what?"

"I saw you and Fonzie Jr exchanging body heat yesterday."

"Oh my god, we were not." My face flushed and the guide slipped from my hands.

Of course Libby would be the one to see us. She was going to have so much fun holding this over me; I could already see the jokes forming in her head.

"It wouldn't be a bad thing, you know," she said, snatching my TV guide from the floor and sinking into the couch. "You're both hot, so why not?"

Well, that was the last thing I expected her to say. Actually, a lot of things Libby had been doing over the past few days were unexpected. It wasn't like her not to tease me ruthlessly about Aiden and what happened in the car.

Or what didn't happen.

It wasn't like I planned to keep it a secret. I just didn't see the point in sharing something that was never going to happen again. Aiden was such an enigma that even if I cared—which I didn't—I wouldn't be able to tell you whether he actually liked me or whether the almost kiss was some sort of temporary insanity.

"I just think you shouldn't write him off completely," Libby cut into my thoughts, her voice muffled from the guide being held too closely to her face. "You've been doing this whole independent 'I don't need no man' thing for way too long."

"There's nothing wrong with being alone."

"As long as you're not lonely," she fired back, tearing a free sample of perfume from the guide and rubbing it over her wrist. "It's okay to be alone, but once you start hating it, it's time to find another warm body to get close to."

Okay, fair point. But I wasn't lonely.

The fact that Libby was so invested in this was suss. She always joked about me finally cashing in my V card all the time and returned my attention to our upcoming meeting with the others.

With a quick glance at the clock, I strained my ears to hear any movement from upstairs. When I could hear nothing but the ticking clock, I stood up and motioned for Libby that it was time to go. She huffed at my refusal to continue our conversation and moved to the door without looking at me.

With Libby in one of her "you're a terrible friend" moods, it was going to be a long night.

I shook my head and followed her out of the front door, locking it as quietly as I could. In my mind, closing the door without detection was like diffusing a temperamental bomb, and if I wasn't careful it was going to explode with a monstrous bang. The bang being a punishment so bad, my parents wouldn't let me see outside my room until graduation.

It was dark outside and the only people in the street were a couple of late night exercise fanatics. The glow from a nearby street lamp was dim and cast a yellow light over the sidewalk. The front lawn was moist with dew and the sky was so cloudy not even the moon was visible.

Libby started walking to the front gates and I reached out to grab her arm.

"Do you really want to risk going out the front gate and having my parents spot us from the window?" My dad constantly got up to use the bathroom at different times throughout the night and we really didn't need him seeing us.

"Good point."

I motioned to the side of the house. It was much safer to go around the back and take the street behind mine to Sasha's house. The previous owner had been an environmentalist who had framed the whole side of the house with shrubbery. It was perfect for decoration but terrible for sneaking out. There was only a small space between the shrubs and the neighbour's fence so we needed to shimmy our way through.

"Ow!" Libby whispered harshly. "Stupid branch."

We fumbled out on the other side and I saw Libby assess the damage. Her ACDC top, which was really just one of my tops that she had "borrowed", had torn where a thread had caught on a branch.

"So much for that outfit."

"Shut up," she groaned, gently brushing a few loose leaves from her skirt.

With a sympathetic smile, I crept forward and took the back gate out onto the road behind us. The only sounds that could be heard over the movement of our feet were the crickets in the grass and a train in the distance. As we spent the next few minutes walking in silence, I took the chance to look around. My neighbourhood was usually noisy with people chatting over their fences and cars going to and from work. However, now it was empty with only the vehicles sitting eerily out front of the homes. The streets were actually somewhat peaceful as Libby and I finally turned into the cul-de-sac where Aiden and Sasha lived.

* * *

Sasha's house really didn't fit the profile of someone who was interested in stealing, with its suburban style front yard and lawn fixtures. We ended up arriving exactly on time and finding Aiden waiting at the front door with a crooked smirk on his face.

"Hello, ladies," he said, closing the door and leading us into the kitchen. He was dressed in his leather jacket, teamed with black cargo pants and a polo shirt, and looking even more smug than usual. Libby was going to love this way too much.

As I gazed over Aiden's body, I shuddered at the memory of what happened in his car. I had avoided his gaze when I first arrived, but with the memory burning into my brain I locked eyes with his.

Something didn't seem right. His eyes were darker than normal, with his pupils large and void of emotion, causing fear to course straight to my heart.

We rounded the corner of the kitchen and entered the living room where everyone was already waiting.

"I think introductions are in order," Aiden announced, pointing to the tall bulky guy who we had seen him with previously. "You ladies already know Greg."

Finally, I had a name to connect to the face. Greg gave us an awkward wave before rambling on about how he was missing out on the footy game for us and that we had better get on with the plan. He didn't seem too smart by the vacant expression on his face, but he seemed harmless enough.

Aiden silenced Greg with a hand on his shoulder before introducing the other two people standing in front of us.

"And these are the brains and the beauty of the group, Noah and Brooke."

Noah raised his hand and saluted us with a dorky grin on his face. He wore a black polo with a tie in the exact same colour. Either wearing a tie with a polo shirt was a new fashion trend I had missed or this boy was all kinds of weird. He was much smaller than the other boys but his posture screamed authority. His skin was like porcelain, and when he smiled his lips darkened and covered his teeth.

"So you must be Miss Edwards." Noah's British accent only made his words sound even more sophisticated. "And of course it's always a pleasure to see you, Miss Michaels."

Libby bit her lip and stared at him.

"You two know each other?" I said. She had her I-want-to-know-what-your-lips-taste-like look, which was surprising since Noah wasn't her usual type.

"Oh yes, Noah always had something to say in our English class last year."

"What can I say? Mrs Bishop is an amateur teacher at best." He winked. "I also couldn't resist getting a laugh out of you either."

That would explain why Libby was so keen on attending that class. The two of them continued to flirt shamelessly until Brooke popped up in front of us.

"I can't believe I'm meeting *the* Nicole Edwards!" The girl Aiden had introduced as Brooke walked closer to me until she was only a foot away. "Aiden's told me so much about you. I'm glad you could make it."

Not only was she invading what little personal space I had, she was also acting like we were going to be the best of friends. I was going to tell her how wrong she was but quickly swallowed my words when I saw the enchanted expression she wore, as if she was experiencing everything for the first time. She also had one of those faces that made her look vaguely familiar. Her smile was the brightest I had ever seen and her face was surrounded by copper red hair.

"Let's not embarrass the man, baby." Greg circled his arms around her waist and propped his chin on her shoulder. "Don't want to cockblock him before he even gets to first base."

"Oh my gosh, Greg, don't be so gross."

Wow, okay, talk about opposites attracting. Greg was built like a tank and would have no issue with carrying bags of stolen stuff, so it was obvious why he was here. Brooke was a mystery though. She gave off a wholesome vibe, even as she continued to tell her boyfriend off for using foul language. Why she was involved with chain store theft, and how she could possibly help, was beyond my comprehension.

I shifted slightly away from the pair and scanned the room, connecting eyes with a pale girl sitting on the couch, whose black hair had been styled into an edgy pixie cut. Maybe "girl" was the wrong word to use. She had to be at least eighteen.

Aiden cleared his throat. "Of course, who could forget the most important introduction of them all?" he said with a hint of sarcasm. "Ladies, meet my sister, Sasha."

The short girl walked closer to us and raised her hands to rest on her hips. She made no move to greet us or shake our hands. Something was obviously stuck up her butt if she was going to hate on us without even knowing us. Whatever she was thinking, it couldn't have been pleasant if the deep scowl on her face was any indication.

With a quick flick of her wrist, she motioned towards the lavish mahogany dining table where Aiden had taken a seat. Libby and I followed her and sat down, facing the Campbell siblings and the others as they joined us.

Aiden wasn't the only one dressed completely in dark colours, they all were. Even Greg wore all black clothing, and I had never seen him in anything that wasn't bright enough to scorch your eyes out if you dared to look long enough.

I glanced back at the kitchen and couldn't see any maps or anything that we would have needed if we were spending the night making plans. That uncomfortable feeling of panic started to grow and I felt a little sick.

Something was wrong. It felt like I was watching a horror movie and couldn't warn the victim that the killer was waiting for them inside the closet.

I turned my attention to the lounge room where Sasha had been sitting earlier, and saw three camping backpacks resting against the couch. They were full to the point where the zipper was threatening to burst. On and around the couch and were old car doors and plastic panels with wires sticking out of them. I couldn't exactly pinpoint what it was but something about that weird collection of items sent a huge jolt through my body. The panic rose in my heart and I gripped Libby's hand painfully tightly under the table. She snapped her head towards me in confusion, but returned the tight grasp regardless.

"What's in the backpacks?" I asked with as much authority as I could muster.

"Oh, you know, the usual," Sasha replied coolly, still staring directly at me and keeping her face emotionless. "Crowbars, screwdrivers, pliers, blah blah blah."

"Why would we need all those items to steal clothes?" I asked slowly. I already knew the answer, but I needed to hear Aiden say it before I could believe it.

"I may have misled you a little on that."

I let go of Libby's hand and tightened my arms around myself in a desperate attempt to keep from verbally attacking him. I knew something was off about this whole thing and it definitely had to be bad if Aiden had chosen to lie to us about it.

"So, we're not here to make plans to steal clothing?" Libby musn't have caught on to how much trouble we were in just yet.

Sasha smiled with a hint of smugness. The look on her face was a mix of amusement, pleasure and something entirely else.

"Well, girls, it seems my dear brother forgot to fill you in on everything," she said in a delighted tone. "We, as in all seven of us, will be going shopping for a few new cars."

This time Libby was the first to catch on to what Sasha really meant. I was still caught up in what Aiden had told us, so when Sasha mentioned cars, I hadn't quite grasped what she meant. It wasn't until I felt Libby's hand clench around my upper arm that I finally caught up. They wanted us to help them steal cars. My eyes bulged at the realisation and I instantly started trying to find a way out. This wasn't *The Fast and the Furious*. We weren't in a Hollywood blockbuster and they were insane to even consider it.

"There's no way we're going to help you," I back-pedalled, dragging Libby up with the hand she had wrapped around my arm and speed walking to the front door. "This is not what we agreed on. Besides, we don't know the first thing about stealing cars."

As soon as I finished my sentence and reached for the door, Greg and Noah wedged themselves in front of us. Libby shrank in on herself and I couldn't blame her. We were the stupid girls in every terrible teen slasher film imaginable. Even though Aiden and his gang didn't seem like the cold-blooded killer type, we weren't prepared to find out.

"Move!" I commanded, slightly surprised by the strength in my voice.

Greg peered behind me to look at Aiden.

This was all his fault. I gave him a glare that would put Draco Malfoy to shame.

"Oh, please don't be like that, Edwards," he said slyly. "You shouldn't be frowning so much or you'll wrinkle that cute face of yours."

He pushed himself up from the chair and came closer until the warmth radiating from his skin seeped into mine. He moved to touch my shoulder but I slapped his hand away. I was so stupid to think there was more to Aiden. He was the same jerk he had always been.

"You can't keep us here," I argued, moving into the kitchen. I knew I was further from the door, but I needed room to breathe and being trapped between two boys was not the place for it.

I tensed as Aiden walked in and leant against the bench opposite me. Libby had returned to her chair and was watching us from across the room. The kitchen had an open bar style design so whatever I had to say wasn't going to be kept between just Aiden and me.

"Don't you understand? We're offering you an opportunity to attempt something that many people can only dream about," Aiden argued. "We're offering you skills beyond your knowledge and a ridiculous amount of money."

"Forget it," I snapped, turning to face him. "I'm not interested."

"You should be."

"What's that supposed to mean?"

"It means that if you don't join us you'll be suspended for cheating on both your English and Maths final exams." Aiden's voice wasn't smooth anymore; it was low and made my heart start thumping louder in that horror-inducing way. "You think Murdoch will want to touch you with a record like that?"

"But I never cheated!"

"That's irrelevant." He shifted slightly. "Noah is top of his IT class. He'd have no problem accessing your file and including a note of your academic indiscretions, as well as sending an email to Murdoch informing them."

I stared at him in disgust. He wouldn't. No one could be that cruel. I had worked my arse off for years to get my straight-A record! Late nights, extra credit essays on boring crap like politics and physics. Then there was the stuff they didn't teach you in class—like knowing how to play the teachers, finding out what was their interests were and exploiting them. I would even choose the right moment to give them a sob story about how much my parents' money problems were keeping me up at night. That seemed pretty ironic now, and not in a good way. No matter how I achieved it though, surely even Aiden wouldn't destroy all my hard work in a single mouse-click.

Of course, I should have known not to think that. His body language told me everything I needed to know. Aiden stood with his elbows against the bench and his foot tapping to an imaginary beat. There wasn't a single molecule of remorse in his eyes and that's what really scared me.

"There's something seriously wrong with you," I spat. "Normal people have lightness and darkness within them but when I look at you, Aiden, all I see is darkness. You're not normal."

He watched me with narrowed eyes as I tried to calm myself down enough to think of a way out of this. Libby looked over my way and I just knew the others were listening in as well. I finally saw Aiden properly for the first time and I couldn't tear my eyes away or dull the ache in my chest.

"So what's it going to be?"

Clenching my fists in a ball, my lips formed a thin line. In my head I rapidly scanned through all the options available, but I couldn't see a way out. I could tell my parents about Aiden's threat, or report it to the school, but even if I could prevent Murdoch thinking I was a cheat, how could I explain how I got myself into this situation in the first place? All Aiden had to do was reveal that he caught me shoplifting and it was game over. The heat had risen from within my stomach and my cheeks flushed. I felt the familiar sting to my eyes and I silently begged myself not to cry.

Before the other day, I thought he was a tool. Now, he was much lower than that.

"Fine, we'll do it," I said, glancing quickly to confirm my decision with Libby. She shrugged because even she knew there was no choice.

"Please understand, Edwards." Aiden pushed himself up from the bench and walked closer to me with a sigh. "I told you I wouldn't let you get hurt and I meant it. Just relax and let yourself enjoy the adventure."

His body visibly relaxed from the semi-tense position he'd been in from the moment we entered the kitchen. Now that he was closer, I could see the light purple bags forming under his eyes that screamed multiple restless nights. Kind of like how I looked after pulling an all-nighter before an exam. He looked much older than he really was and his curls weren't as tamed as they usually were. He straightened his back and started to walk towards the living room to join the others.

"Why are you doing this?"

He stopped and turned to look at me. His eyes had returned to their emptiness and his mouth dropped a little. "We all have someone to answer to," he whispered. "You're not the only one with limited options."

With that, he left the kitchen with his smirk back in place and his hands in his jacket pockets. There was no option B for Libby and me. We were going to be stealing cars that night whether we wanted to or not.

7
The Plan

Never in my life had I been so confused by another person. I was getting a chronic headache from the constant back and forth between Aiden's emotions. I didn't realise I was part of a twisted tennis match, where one moment he was flirting and the next he was blackmailing me to join his group.

After a few moments had passed and I no longer felt like punching Aiden in the face, I left the kitchen and joined the others in the lounge room. They all tried to pretend they hadn't heard us but obviously they were terrible actors. Each of them avoided my eyes, except for Brooke who just stared blankly. Noah stood up swiftly, clearing his throat and placing a map in front of us.

"Okay, so now that we're all in," he glanced at me apologetically before continuing, "this is what we're after."

The map was an aerial shot of the entire town and every detail imaginable was included. They had even added the new community garden that the workers had only completed last week.

I stared at the industrial district section, which had three small red pins placed on Fairview Drive, the street with the most blacked out warehouses on the map. I hadn't been to the place before, but that wasn't surprising since I tended to avoid the industrial district as much as I could. Everyone knew that nothing good ever happened there.

"I've spent the day watching our targets and they haven't moved at all," Noah explained. "These pins represent the exact location of the cars and the neon ones represent us."

In a little container next to the map were seven different coloured pins. They hadn't been placed on the map yet, but before I could ask anything Brooke started picking a colour for each person. She gave me the green one because, according to her, green was the colour of happiness, not yellow.

I was going to get along just great with her.

"So what's the plan?" Greg asked. "I know I'm here because I'm good with my hands and because we've been bros since primary school, but I'm not good with plans, dude."

Aiden raised his hand to silence Greg. "That's what Edwards is for."

I tore my eyes from the pins and frowned at Aiden. It was foolish to think I'd get away with being a tag along. Planning was what Aiden wanted me for, after all. With a quick glance at the group around me, I exhaled in exasperation and moved closer to the map.

"It's going to be easier if we work in teams." Slowly the map started to come alive. Instead of red pins, I could see three Mitsubishi Lancers. I saw the warehouses unevenly lining the perimeter of the district and their distance from the entrance of the street. Noah slid next to me and watched my hand trace the path of the first pin.

"That one's going to be tricky," he commented. "It's the only one with a wheel lock on it. We might be able to break the lock but it's going to take time."

"Sasha might be able to pick the lock." Aiden glanced at his sister. "She went through a spy stage when we were younger. She got pretty at it too."

"Fine, Sasha can handle it but I want someone else to go with her."

Noah nodded and placed a neon pin next to the car. Brooke was chosen to go with Sasha and help her with the equipment.

Greg tensed at the news, only relaxing when Brooke placed a comforting hand on his back. Clearly, he didn't like the idea of being separated from her very much.

"The second car is jammed tightly between two other cars so you're going to need to take the break off and push it out before you start it."

Greg was obviously going to be a part of that group. The bulging muscles under his shirt sleeves and the thickness of his chest were enough to confirm he was strong. With the second car being the trickiest, Noah and Libby were also teamed up with him. That left just Aiden and me to work on the third car. I glanced at Libby and was confused to see anger flash across her face briefly. I couldn't tell if she was angry because this would be the first time we were going to be separated or because of something else entirely.

Either way, I was just as angry. I wasn't sure if I could work with someone I didn't trust, let alone how I was going to go about it.

"I guess that means Aiden and I are taking care of the third car then." I was not impressed one bit. "It's the closest to our exit so we'll be leading everyone out."

Noah stuck our individual pins into their appropriate places and gave everyone a chance to memorise their positions. I studied each person and tried to work out why they were there. I knew what Libs and I were doing there, but I also knew Greg came from a wealthy family. He didn't need the money and I doubt he was being blackmailed since he didn't seem tense, only bored. As for Brooke, I couldn't see her motive at all, so she had to be in because of Greg or for something else. I couldn't figure out Aiden and Sasha's situation either. I had never met their parents, not even at parent-teacher nights. Sometimes I wondered if they even had any.

Everyone else was still studying the map. They all seemed to accept the plans for the heist without questioning them, even Libby. How were they missing the one glaring problem?

"Excuse me," I said scowling at Aiden. "I think we might be forgetting one tiny detail." The others looked at me in anticipation, expecting some new mastermind idea. "I'm only on my Learners with limited driving experience, guys. I barely know how to parallel park let alone how to break into a car, or start it without a key. Neither does Libby." I glanced at her for confirmation. She gave a little shrug as if to say, sure, it might be a bit tricky.

To my surprise, it was Brooke who answered. "Don't worry, Noah says it's as easy as playing *Grand Theft Auto*."

What on earth was she on about?

Noah stepped forward, with that dark smile pasted against his pale skin, the one that Libby couldn't take her eyes off.

"Brooke's right, you'll all be masters by the time I'm done teaching you the dark arts of vehicle purloining. Your classroom lies over there." He gestured with his hand towards the car doors and plastic panels over by the sofa.

Clearly they had put a lot of thought into this. It seemed it wasn't the first time they had done something like this. Or at least not the first time they had planned it.

"So, questions?" Aiden asked, looking at all of us and clasping his hands together.

"I have one," Noah said, shifting in his chair. "I know who's with whom but what's the game plan?"

"I thought that would have been obvious," Sasha said coldly. She walked over to the map and pointed to Fairview Drive's adjoining street. "We're going to enter through here before splitting up."

That didn't seem right. Surely the others could see that if we entered via the street, we'd be out in the open. We might as well call the cops ourselves. I scanned the map with a frown as the others broke off into conversation. There had to be another way.

Running my eyes across the map again, I spotted just what I needed, a side street passageway. It was only faintly printed on the map but it was a much better option.

"We can't take the main entrance, it's too dangerous," I stated, catching everyone's attention.

Sasha's eyes darkened to a dangerous colour. "Excuse me?"

"I said we can't take the entrance onto Fairview. We should take the passageway adjacent to the street. It'll give us the coverage we need."

Before Sasha could argue, Aiden had agreed and continued to explain the rest of the plan. We would stay close until we exited the passageway, then we'd separate. Sasha and Brooke would go left towards their car while the boys and Libby would go right. Aiden and I were going to keep walking straight to where our car would be waiting. Sasha glared at me the entire time Aiden spoke. Honestly, she was giving me the creeps.

No matter how much planning we did though, there was still no denying it: this was going to end very badly. My stomach twisted painfully as I closed my eyes and breathed in. When did my life become the plot for *Gone in Sixty Seconds*?

With the others wearing freakishly calm expressions, I wasn't sure if they even knew how serious this was. Either they were all on drugs or they were really good at faking. No way were they naturally that relaxed.

"Right, now that we have the information sorted, it's time for the equipment," Noah added. "We've got all the tools that are needed for the Porsches in these bags."

He distributed a backpack to each group and they were surprisingly much heavier than I thought. I held on tightly to the strap and frowned.

"Wait, we're doing this for a couple of Porsches?"

"A couple of Porsches?" Greg scoffed. "Is this chick serious?"

He gave me a bewildered look and placed a hand on his forehead, rubbing small circles into the skin. That was the first time Greg had looked annoyed and the first time I hadn't heard him say "dude".

"Edwards, these aren't just any Porsches," Aiden added with that arrogant tone that reminded me just how angry I was at him. "These are 2015 Porsche Panamera Hybrids. They're top of the line."

"Yeah, they are Porsche royalty," Greg said, passion lighting his eyes. "The Panamera's an eight speed automatic with a turbocharged petrol-electric hybrid engine with a rev range of 6000rpm, man. They are not just *some Porsche.* The owners must be filthy rich if they just leave these babies lying around out there."

I stared at the boys, blankly trying to make sense of what they had just said. I wasn't a stranger to cars and I could appreciate a beautiful vehicle as much as the next person, but as soon as someone started describing the features, I felt like I was trying to understand another language.

"Yep, we've lost her." Aiden laughed, lightly brushing a hand against my shoulder. A shiver ran down my spine and I tried to ignore it. He might be able to pretend that nothing was wrong between us but I certainly couldn't. "Let's just say these cars are extremely expensive and leave it at that."

I narrowed my eyes and sank back into the couch, awaiting my turn for a lesson with Noah. The sooner we did this, the sooner I could forget all about it—and all about Aiden.

Maybe because I looked so unapproachable, scowling on the couch, I was the last to get my training. I stifled a yawn as Noah called me over. On one side of the couch, Greg and Brooke were working on a car door together, while on the other side Libby fiddled with wires, her lips pursed in concentration as if it was some maths puzzle she hadn't done the homework for. I had to give it to her though; she certainly had nimble fingers as she worked the multi-coloured wires.

Noah guided me over to the car door in front of us. "We'll start with breaking the lock. That's the easy bit," he said, handing me a slim metal hook. "Just slide it down the side of the glass until you find the lock pin, then give it a gentle pull." He demonstrated for me, and the plastic lock button inside the car shot up. Noah pushed it back down again.

"Now you try." I took the hook from him. Sliding it down the side of the window wasn't too hard, but after that I was lost. I couldn't see what Noah had been doing once the tool was inside the car door. I jiggled the hook around uselessly for a couple of minutes, getting more and more frustrated, until Noah took my hand in his cold, slim fingers.

"The pin is here, near the handle," he said. He moved my hand until I felt the hook catch on something. "Then just pull ..." The lock button popped up, and despite myself, I smiled. Maybe I could do this after all!

"Okay, let's move on to getting the car started." Noah pulled a plastic panel towards us. "First you need to remove the panel under the steering wheel with a screwdriver. Here's one I prepared earlier," he grinned, pulling the front of the panel off. "So you take this wire here ..."

I tried to concentrate as he showed me which wires to strip, which ones to connect, and which ones to avoid. I wasn't planning a life as a car thief, but nor was I planning on getting caught because I couldn't start the car I had to steal. My whole plan for my life depended on getting through tonight without anyone ever finding out.

Actually, it didn't look that hard. I'd always been pretty good at electrical circuits in Physics, so this didn't faze me. When Noah reset the wires and handed the panel over to me, I got it right the first time.

"Excellent!" said Noah, exactly as if he was a real teacher. "You keep practising. I'm going to go and help Brooke."

I tried the wires one more time, but I was pretty sure I'd got the hang of it, so I went back to the door. That was much harder. The damn lock pin was tiny! I fished around like an idiot, starting to get really frustrated, when warm fingers closed firmly over mine and guided my hand down and slightly to the left.

"It's next to the inside handle," Aiden said. I pulled my hand away as if it was burnt.

"Only trying to help, Edwards," he said, smirking.

"If you wanted to help you could try not blackmailing me into stealing cars," I hissed at him. His eyes immediately went cold, so cold that *I* got chills, but at least he turned and left me alone. Trying to concentrate, I pushed the lock button down and started again.

* * *

It was close to two in the morning by the time we had finished. Everyone had taken turns with Noah, except Aiden and Sasha who already seemed to know everything they needed, and then we practised and practised until we were confident. Libby was in the kitchen with Greg, getting yet another demonstration from Noah on how to break into a car door. Oh yeah, I was sure she was *deeply* interested in the workings of locks, and not at all in Noah's cute butt as he leaned over the door.

I sat in the lounge with my legs tucked tightly underneath me, pulling the backpack onto my lap. Dragging the zipper open slowly, almost as if the bag contained a bomb, I looked inside. Packed snuggly were more tools than I imagined we'd ever need. Honestly, what on earth were we going to do with rope? Drag the cars out?

Underneath the rope, there were an assortment of pliers

and screwdrivers in all sizes. On top of the tools sat a large metal hook.

"It's to jimmy the lock with," Brooke said, sitting down next to me. I nodded in agreement. My hands were sore from practising with it. "Although, I don't know who Jimmy is exactly," she added.

She frowned slightly in confusion. She reminded me so much of a child who was trying to work out her maths timetables. It almost didn't seem logical that someone so innocent was involved in this.

I almost missed the two soft rectangle shapes wrapped in foil. "What's this?"

"Sandwiches," she replied, placing her bag next to mine. "I packed two in each bag just in case we were hungry. Mum always does it for Dad when he's working on the farm."

The farm? A memory drifted into my mind of learning to ride a horse when I was a kid, at the Henleys' place. It was a horse-breeding farm, the only one in Silverlake. Suddenly I realised why Brooke looked familiar. The Henleys had a daughter who was home schooled until recently. Her arrival at Sterling High was huge news since we rarely got new students.

I guess that would explain why she acted so angelic. It wasn't hard to see why they had decided to home school Brooke. She seemed so unaware of danger, so caught up in her own imaginary world—the kind of person who could be easily damaged by the real world. I envied her. Sometimes I wished I could see the world the way she did. I wished I could see it as a place of beauty and not something that could leave you cold and jaded if you weren't careful.

Instead of trying to question Brooke, I just nodded at her and returned to fiddling with the backpack. With every second that passed it was getting harder to focus. Dread and adrenaline rose in the pit of my stomach.

"This is your first time doing something like this, isn't it?" Brooke said, smiling in encouragement.

"Is it that obvious?"

She laughed softly and placed a hand on my arm. "You don't need to worry," she replied. "We're a family so we take care of each other. Nothing's going to happen to you, promise."

"Why are you here?" I blurted. "What do you get from this?"

Thankfully she wasn't insulted by my random question. Instead she frowned, looking so sad that I would've preferred if she was angry because at least then she wouldn't be giving me puppy dog eyes.

"I don't exactly know what happened but the police said my identity was stolen. All I did was go online shopping, so I'm not sure how someone got hold of my bank account or how they managed to drain it." She looked in the direction of the others. "I told Aiden what happened and he said he'd help me get my money back if I helped him pick up some cars for their new owner."

Things were starting to make sense. If I understood her correctly, it seemed like Brooke had accidentally messed with a spam website. Greg's involvement made sense as well. He wouldn't let his girlfriend go into this without him. The part that I didn't understand was why Aiden wanted to help her. Unless Brooke was a genius in disguise or fast with her hands, Aiden had no use for her.

I turned my attention toward him. He was talking to Noah with an intense expression etched on his face. It seemed like every time I thought I knew Aiden, I would discover something about him that would throw me completely off balance.

"He's not that bad, you know."

I snapped my attention back to Brooke. She must've been watching me the whole time since her smile was so wide I could almost count every tooth in her mouth.

"What?"

"Aiden," she clarified. "I know he did a mean thing to you, but he's never usually like that. Unlocking these cars is just really important to him."

As I opened my mouth to question her, Aiden called us all into the lounge. I stood up as everyone entered the room and swung the backpack over my shoulder. With my internal panic kicking in, there wasn't much time to ponder Aiden's motives. It was time to get this done and never think about it again.

"Okay, this is it guys. There's no turning back now," Noah said, grabbing a backpack and signalling to Sasha to do the same. "We've only got an hour to get there, take the Porsches and get out. So no matter what, don't mess about."

Brooke stood up and dusted off her pants as the others filed out into the driveway. "Well, it's a beautiful night for stealing cars."

She held her hand out to me and it dampened my nerves just enough that I could keep my hands from trembling. That would be embarrassing and I didn't need the others knowing that I was far from ready. Giving a small smile in return, I let her lead the way out to the others. Just like Libby, Brooke seemed to know when I needed a little comfort, and I was incredibly grateful.

The darkness of the night surrounded us as we started the walk to Fairview Drive in silence.

8
This is it

Fairview Drive was eerily quiet when we arrived. There was only one building with lights on but as it was a few warehouses down from where the cars sat we knew we wouldn't be bothered.

We emerged from the side alleyway and paused just before the street lamp could reveal us. The Porsches were exactly where Noah indicated they'd be.

Greg smirked proudly. "Brooke and I have been scoping the place out all day," he whispered. "They haven't moved once."

I took in the three different coloured Porsches parked along the street. To the right was a blood red Porsche that shimmered slightly in the moonlight. I almost missed the Porsche on my left. Its black paint job blended in so well with the darkness that I probably would've walked straight into it if I hadn't known it was supposed to be there.

It was the car that Aiden and I were after that really made my eyes widen. Right in front of us was a Porsche in the most beautiful shade of royal purple that I had ever seen. The car's rims caught the reflection of the street lamp and shimmered as if it had come straight from the dealership. I wondered if it had that new car smell that cars this flash always seemed to have.

The sound of my own gulp was enough to bring me back to our situation. I still couldn't believe Libby and I had managed to get caught up in this mess. There were so many emotions running through my head that I wasn't exactly sure how I should've felt. All I knew was that once this was done, I was never going to look at Aiden again. Anger was still pulsating through me and every time I saw him, all I wanted to do was yell until my throat was raw.

I felt a hand brush against my elbow and I tensed, thinking it was Aiden. He had an annoying habit of appearing at exactly the same time that I was thinking about him. Only this time it was Libby.

"Chill out, it'll be okay," she said just loud enough for me to hear. "This is what we want."

I had no idea what that was supposed to mean. This wasn't what I wanted at all. What I wanted was to be at home and in my comfy bed. Not here, gearing up to steal cars. I turned to tell Libby just that, but her expression stopped me. She was weirdly calm and her body was relaxed.

Something wasn't adding up. No one was ever that calm before doing something illegal. Well, maybe Aiden, but he was basically evil in human form, so he didn't count. Why was Libby okay with this when I was freaking out?

"Okay everyone, it's time to separate." Aiden's voice cut through the group's silence. "We'll be meeting the buyers as soon as we are done here so don't mess around. You have twenty minutes to get the car and get out of here. We'll be meeting up near Merchant's Alley where it's safe so don't waste time. Good luck."

Libby disappeared from my side and followed the boys towards the red Porsche.

Brooke gripped my hand quickly and then raced off to the black Porsche with Sasha trailing behind her.

"You ready, Edwards?" Aiden whispered into my ear from behind. "Don't worry, I'll keep you safe."

Sure he would. He would have been more believable if he wasn't the reason why I was there in the first place. I bit my lip to stop myself from lashing out at him even though I really wanted to. This wasn't the time to be angry. I needed my full attention to be solely on the Porsche sitting in front of us.

"Let's just get this done."

Aiden dipped his head in a quick nod and then led the way towards the car. We ran quickly until we were beside the driver's door.

"Okay, Edwards, this is the tricky part." I frowned at Aiden as he walked towards the hood of the car. "I'm going to pull the alarm wires at the same time as you open the door, otherwise get ready for some high pitched screeching."

He couldn't be serious.

No way.

Oh god, he was. This wasn't mentioned in training.

Aiden immediately took the bag from my shoulder and pulled out the metal rod. He carefully slotted the jimmy between the hood and the base of the car. With a quick jerk, he snapped the lock and lifted the hood.

"Ready?"

Nope. No way. Definitely not. Not even close. Who could ever be ready for this?

With a deep breath, I took the jimmy from his hands and slid it tentatively between the window and the car door. I needed to unlock the door before we got anywhere near trying to disable the alarm. Pressing down slightly, I fiddled with the rod until a tiny click sound was heard.

"All right." Placing my hand on the car door, I connected eyes with Aiden and he counted down from three.

Now I know why people always panicked about that. Was I supposed to pull the door open when Aiden got to one or did I open it when he said go? My hands started to shake and I wished I had just asked Aiden before he started counting, but he reached one and before I could doubt myself anymore, I screwed my eyes shut and pulled the door handle. I could have sworn that my heart stopped at that moment. Thankfully, the only sound I could hear was our staggered breathing.

"That's it, baby," he said with a grin. "Unlock for us."

Of course Aiden was one of those guys who referred to their cars as "baby". Closing my eyes and breathing out in relief, I pulled the car door fully open.

Holy cow, the Porsche was just as beautiful on the inside as it was on the outside. The seats were beige leather that was smooth to touch and the steering wheel was the perfect distance from the seats.

"Are you stealing the car or making love to it?" Aiden said with a smirk.

"Shut up."

I ran my hand across the space just below the steering wheel as I tried to remember everything Noah had shown me. My fingers grazed across the clip that held the access cover in place.

"Pass the flat-head screwdriver, please," I asked Aiden, who was still holding the backpack. He placed the screwdriver into my outstretched hand and I jammed it at the clip.

I should've known that I would miss it completely and end up slicing my finger open. I wouldn't even play sports at school because I was such a klutz. Hissing in pain, I quickly retracted my finger and wrapped it in the hem of my shirt.

"You okay?" Aiden asked over my shoulder. "I can do that if you can't."

"I can do it."

I wasn't about to show weakness, especially not to Aiden. Removing my finger from my shirt, I could tell that I was in desperate need of a Band-Aid, but I could work without the finger for now. Switching the screwdriver into my injured hand, I used my other one to feel for the clip again. This time with a little caution, I jammed the screwdriver into the clip, separating the access cover from the steering wheel.

I pulled out the wires and tried to find the two that looked the same. I didn't realise there would be so many of them. Literally dozens of wires spread from the clip into different areas of the car and I couldn't tell them apart. There had been nowhere near this many in Noah's demonstration model.

"They're the red ones," Aiden pointed out, passing me pliers. "Cut the ends and tape them together."

I wanted to tell him to back off, especially when he was practically leaning against me to see into the car, but I kept quiet. He was right about the wires, and as much as I'd have liked to tell him to leave it to me, he knew this a lot better than I did.

"If you're going to back-seat drive me on this then maybe we should switch."

"Then how will you ever learn?"

Breathing in deeply, I attempted to get a grip on my annoyance. Just as I had taken the two wires out from their clip as Aiden had instructed, a high-pitched screeching filled the air. I fumbled with the wires and looked at Aiden in panic.

"Crap, someone's tripped an alarm." He added quickly, "It's not us," reassuring me slightly.

"What do we do?" I screeched.

Aiden looked into my eyes and his features softened before he did something I hadn't been expecting. He lifted his hand and massaged my arm before his face morphed back into business mode.

"Go," he answered. "I'll finish this one up and bring it to you. Find out who has the alarm and help them."

I felt better with a plan in place, so I switched positions with Aiden and ran towards the noise.

"Nic, over here," Brooke called out. "The car won't stop screaming."

I hurried over to the wailing car and saw Brooke attempting to hotwire it without success. The Porsche's indicators were blinking and the car was one big flashing sign alerting every-one to our presence.

"What happened?"

"I used the jimmy on it but it mustn't have liked that," she replied in a panic. "I don't know how to stop it."

She dug through her bag and pulled out random pliers to try to cut the wire that was sending the alarm into full alert. I could see panic filling her face, but I couldn't blame her because I knew I had the same expression mirrored on mine. The alarm hadn't been going for very long but that didn't matter. I was ter-rified that the owners would be on their way—or even worse, they might be calling the police. I needed to shake off my fear and come up with something quick.

Brooke kept pulling different tools out of the bag in her frantic attempts to stop the alarm. I was about to tell her to give it up and get out of here when a shimmer of light caught my attention. I looked down and saw the wrapped sandwich lying on the floor, half squished by the backpack.

An idea came into my mind and before I was aware of what I was doing, I had scooped up the sandwich and torn off the foil, pushing Brooke out of the way.

I wasn't sure if it would work since I generally didn't pay much attention in science class, but it was worth a try. I grabbed the ignition wires and wrapped them tightly with the foil. Instantly the alarm cut off and I exhaled in relief.

"What did you do?" Brooke asked her voice rough and shaken.

"I used the foil to restore the electronic current to the lock system," I explained, walking to the front of the car to shut the hood. "The car will think it's locked so the alarm will no longer go off when you touch it."

Brooke stared at me for a moment before smiling brightly. "I knew those sandwiches would come in handy." She laughed, pulling me into a hug.

I laughed with her and felt the tension melt out of my body. So much had happened and we needed to hurry, but being engulfed in a bear hug was so calming that it took me a few moments to assess everything.

"Hey," I asked once we broke apart. "Where's Sasha?"

"She left," Brooke replied, her eyes darkening. "She said she needed to see some people on her own."

What the hell? Sasha was the most interested one of us all; there was no way she would just drop out in the middle of it.

"Nic?"

"What?"

"I think we should start moving if we want to go home."

I nodded and started to walk back to the front seat when I heard a loud crack. It was kind of like someone had hit the mute button. Everything went eerily silent. I spun around and saw Brooke standing where I was before, frozen in place. I wasn't sure what the sound was at first, convinced it was a car backfiring somewhere. I looked down at myself and everything was fine, but Brooke was still standing motionless.

"Oh," she said finally, looking down at her own body.

My eyes followed hers and widened when I saw a thick red stain expand from her chest. It started to leak down until a small puddle of blood formed. Brooke fell to the ground moments later, unnaturally pale.

Thump. Thump. Thump. Thump. My heart was beating so loudly it was all I could hear. I felt like I was submerged under water and everything was muffled. I'd watched enough *Die Hard* movies to know that Brooke had just been shot, but I wasn't prepared for how instead of slowing down, time sped up so fast that I felt like I was about to pass out. The ringing in my ears that began after the loud crack started to fade and my focus returned.

Oh god.

The pool of blood around Brooke had doubled and was seeping around my shoes. I could smell the rusty metallic scent of Brooke's blood and knew I needed to run or something.

Why the hell wouldn't my legs work?

My breathing sped up and just as I went to scream, a rough hand covered my mouth, muffling any noise.

I wasn't ready to die. I had to get away from here.

As I attempted to push the person off of me, a familiar voice breathed into my ear.

"Relax, it's me," Aiden whispered. "I'm not going to hurt you."

The tension in my body eased up a bit as he pulled me down behind the Porsche. He kept glancing towards the lit building. I copied him, and saw the faint shadows of people rustling about.

"What's going on?" I whispered harshly, holding the tears back. "Who the hell are these people?

"We've been tricked," he said, pulling me close and dragging me away from the car. "They're not the usual car owners, not if they are willing to kill."

"Where are we going?" I asked as he continued to move me further from the car and Brooke. She was so pale and still that my eyes started stinging with the start of tears.

Why would anyone shoot at us? They were just cars.

It should have been me instead. A few seconds earlier and the bullet would have gone through me and not Brooke. It just wasn't fair.

"We've got to get the others and get out of here," he replied, pulling me from my thoughts and pushing me into the purple Porsche. "I need to get you somewhere safe."

I was so focused on what had happened that I hadn't noticed the Porsche humming idly. Aiden must have hotwired it while I was helping Brooke.

My tears finally began to fall. Things like this only ever happened in movies, not in real life and especially not to people like Brooke. She was so innocent. How were we going to explain this to everyone?

Oh god, we had to tell Greg.

I lifted my gaze to Aiden and saw the determination in his eyes. The only thing betraying his calm exterior was the death grip he had on the steering wheel that was turning his knuckles white. He was just as scared as I was, no matter how hard he tried to hide it.

* * *

By the time we reached the others, they were all on edge. Greg was sitting in the driver's seat of his idling Porsche, while Noah stood by Libby with his hand on her back for comfort. They each looked like they would be sick any minute. I couldn't blame them. I was freaking out as well.

Aiden stopped abruptly in front of them and we climbed out of the car. There hadn't been any more movement from the building since the gunshot had gone off, which had to be a bad thing.

"What the hell, dude?" Greg asked, panic pulling on his facial features. "Not really the time for a burnout is it?"

Aiden opened his mouth to reply, but Libby walked over to me and placed her hands on my cheeks, trying to get me to focus on her. It hadn't taken more than a second for her to figure out that something was wrong.

Everyone's eyes turned to me when neither Aiden nor I said anything. I opened my mouth to at least try but nothing seemed to come out. It was like any form of communication was trapped in my throat.

"Sunshine?" she questioned, tilting her head to look into my eyes. "What's wrong? What happened?"

She let a shaking hand find its way to my wrist but I flinched and ripped my arm away to curl it around my aching stomach. My tummy was twisting so tightly that I was going to throw up if I didn't calm down soon. I couldn't even close my eyes without seeing Brooke's face permanently etched in surprise.

"Wait." Greg's voice cut through the silence. "Where's Brooke?"

That did it. I moved a few spaces away and emptied my stomach. Libby patted me on the back as I tried to settle down enough to breathe, but I could barely feel her.

"What the hell happened?" she asked Aiden.

"Brooke had a bit of trouble with her car so Edwards went to help her," he said in a strangely calm voice. "I heard the gunshot just as I got to where they were."

"Gunshot?" Greg said, the colour fading from his face. "So where's Brooke?"

The group fell silent and I tilted my head to look at Greg. Everyone knew what Aiden was trying to say, but no one wanted to say it out loud, as if we could somehow change what happened by staying silent. Libby tightened her grip on my back and I felt her hands start to tremble. New tears formed in my eyes and I pawed desperately at them. I couldn't keep crying. Tears weren't going to help any of us.

Aiden gave an unyielding look at Greg and the realisation dawned on him. He went stiff in his seat and the light faded from his eyes.

"No," he said, refusing to look at us. "No you're wrong. I just held her like twenty minutes ago. She was only away from me for a few minutes."

His downcast eyes flicked back and forth, trying to make sense of what Aiden had said. I stood up straight and accepted the bottle of water that Libby had brought along. My mouth was dry and my throat was sore. Noah came over to put an arm around both of us. I didn't know how much I needed that contact until I felt a safe arm around me.

"Greg, I'm sorry," Aiden said, moving towards him and putting a hand on his shoulder. "Someone shot her."

Greg was still for a moment before lunging out of the car and grabbing hold of Aiden's leather jacket, shoving him against the side of the car.

"Shut up," he shouted into his face. "You don't know anything."

Aiden raised his hands to show Greg he meant no harm. Noah reached over and was in the process of trying to pry Greg's hands from Aiden when another shot filled the air.

Not again. Everyone froze and turned towards the lit building. Three figures were moving in the shadows, shouting things that I couldn't quite make out over the distance.

"We have to get out of here," Aiden shouted, pushing Greg off him and towards the back seat of the red Porsche. "Where's Sasha?"

"What do you mean?" Noah shot back, dragging us towards the car. "Wasn't she with Brooke?"

"Brooke said she disappeared right before the alarm went off," I finally choked out, pulling Libby towards the purple Porsche. "We have to go now, Aiden."

He looked torn between looking for his sister and getting as far away as we could from there. Noah threw himself into the red Porsche and hit the accelerator, speeding down the street. The figures were getting closer now and any minute they would be close enough to see us.

Once Libby had dragged herself into the back seat, I hurried over to Aiden's side and grabbed his wrist, pulling him towards the car.

"I can't just leave without her," he said, turning towards me. "What if they have her or she's injured?"

I gently cupped my hand over his mouth, muffling his rambling. He focused on me and for the first time I saw panic in his eyes.

"I know Aiden," I said, pleading with him. "But we can't do anything for her now. We have to go or they are going to kill us."

I felt my pulse thumping—the longer we spent here, the closer the gunmen would get to us. Aiden must have felt my fear because he pulled me to the passenger side, ripping the door open and helping me inside before slamming it shut.

"Okay," he said, "let's get out of here."

Aiden fell into the driver's seat and pulled the door shut, revving the engine and jabbing his foot so hard on the accelerator that I felt my ear drums pop.

"What are we going to do now?" I asked once we had put Fairview Drive a fair distance behind us.

Aiden tore down the road so fast that I had to grip tightly onto the hand rest to stop from strangling myself with the seatbelt.

"I'll tell you what we're doing," he said in a voice I hadn't heard before. "I'm going to drop you two off at your house so your parents won't wake up and freak out when they can't find you."

"But …"

"No, there's nothing else you can do," he said. "Go home, sleep, watch movies … do whatever you usually do."

The rest of the ride was spent in silence. Aiden was adamant that we were to go straight home. My thoughts wandered back to Brooke and I briefly considered calling the police since that was the right thing to do. Except this wasn't a normal situation. We couldn't call the cops without getting caught ourselves. My stomach did a sickly somersault at the thought. I was so far in that I couldn't even call the police to help.

Brooke was gone; there was no way around that. She was the sweetest of us all and we had just left her there on the ground. I felt the bile rise in my stomach and it took all my strength not to throw up again.

"Here we are," Aiden said as he pulled up a few doors down from my house.

"What now?"

"Now you go and try to sleep," he replied. "I'll call you tomorrow to check in on you."

I nodded stiffly and slid out of my seat, too tired to be concerned about anything but getting inside and burying my head under my bedcovers.

Shutting the door behind me and watching Aiden drive off, I felt Libby's hand wrap around my waist and lead me towards my house.

Once inside, I separated from Libby and shuffled into my room. Without the energy to change, I laid my head down and silently begged for sleep to take over. The whole scene kept replaying in my head like it was stuck on some kind of loop. The blood around Brooke grew until it was a few inches from enveloping my feet. I was able to move my feet quickly enough to avoid soaking up the blood but I couldn't stop staring at the puddle. I hadn't noticed the tears until I tasted the saltiness on my lips. I really felt like I would never stop crying and would eventually die from dehydration.

Well, so be it. I deserved it. If I had only silenced that alarm earlier or hadn't stopped to ask questions. If I had been smarter, Brooke would still be here. I curled up into a ball and let the fear and pain take over. The bed shook violently as I tried to muffle my sobs.

"Nicky?" I heard Libby whisper from the doorway.

I hadn't heard her come in, but once she realised I was awake she crept over to the bed and looked down at me.

"I couldn't sleep," she said, and I could see she felt guilty too. I don't really know why she felt guilty; it wasn't her fault, it was mine.

I knew why she was here. She'd be too proud to admit it

but whenever we had a hard time sleeping in primary school, we'd share a bed. Having someone next to us kept the monsters out of our dreams and the fear at bay. We may not be in primary school anymore, but the monsters would no doubt make a reappearance.

Without hesitation, I shuffled over, opening the bed covers and patting the mattress. She slid in and pulled the covers up all the way, until it was tucked under our chins. We didn't speak any further, but I felt a little calmer with her there.

I continued to cry silently until eventually I was all cried out and there was nothing more to give.

9
Last Warning

My phone started buzzing the *Harry Potter* theme song somewhere nearby. After the night I'd had, the sound was pure bliss to my ears. I spent the last couple of hours fighting sleep so that I wouldn't see Brooke's face in my dreams. Even with Libby beside me, I couldn't stop the weight in my lungs from threatening to suffocate me. My muscles were numb from being tense all night and I felt sticky from the cold sweats that kept breaking out over my body.

I shifted in bed and felt across the floor for my phone. When my fingers finally nudged the base of it, I picked it up and tapped the screen open. A text message from a number I didn't recognise took up the entire screen.

I'm coming to get you now. Meet me outside in 20—Aiden.

Squinting at the screen I checked the time and realised it wasn't even six in the morning yet. Aiden had only dropped us off a few hours ago so whatever he was coming to see me about, it wasn't going to be good.

Slipping silently out of bed, I grabbed the first pair of jeans and button up blouse that I could find. I didn't have the energy to worry about how I looked so I just pulled my hair up into a loose bun and pocketed my phone. I glanced over at Libby. Sleeping peacefully, she looked just like the Libs I knew. Not like the girl who was freaking me out by being super calm about stealing cars and then getting angry about doing it in separate groups. Dealing with another unpredictable reaction wasn't something I could handle just now. Making sure I didn't wake Libby up, I crept out of the room.

A few minutes later as I locked the front door, Aiden pulled up in his Lancer. I kept my head down and climbed into the passenger seat, paying extra attention to my seatbelt.

"You've been crying," Aiden stated as he lifted my head and placed his hand gingerly against my cheek.

"No I haven't." I broke eye contact with him and focused on his chest as he exhaled. I don't know what was wrong with me. I just kept staring at his body as it rose and fell with every breath and thinking that Brooke would never be able to do that again. I needed to get a hold of myself before I fell apart completely.

"Come on," he replied softly. "Don't lie to me, Edwards. I can see the tear stains." He gently wiped under my eyes. Pulling my focus from his chest, I raised my eyes to meet his. With a small smile, he started rubbing soothing circles onto my cheek.

My face flushed with anger. Brooke was dead and all he cared about was touching me and pretending that everything was okay. Everything was not okay.

I slapped his hand away abruptly and backed up until I was resting against the window. "Don't."

"What's wrong?"

Was he being serious right now? The very possibility that he could pretend like he didn't know, after everything we went through, was just insane.

"You can't be serious," I exclaimed. "Brooke is dead. What about that don't you get?"

"Why are you yelling at me?" Aiden asked.

"Maybe because you are the reason this all happened."

"You were the one who was with Brooke," he retorted, his eyes ablaze. "Sometimes bad things happen."

I bit my lip to the point where it almost bled, just to control the anger flaring inside me. "I didn't ask for this," I yelled, fresh tears starting to pool in my eyes. I wasn't even sure where this was all coming from. I had opened the seal to everything I had bottled up since the start of this and now all the emotions were pouring out.

"You think I did?" he asked. "You think any of us did?"

"It was your idea, wasn't it?" I fired back. "You wanted to be the bad boy, didn't you? You seriously did all this for a little bit of cash?"

I saw a change in Aiden that I never expected to see. The fire in his eyes was snuffed out almost immediately and he moved back into his seat, dropping his shoulders from their tense position. For the first time, I saw more than arrogance in Aiden.

"I didn't have a choice, Edwards," he replied quietly after a short pause. "I wasn't kidding when I said that we all had someone to answer to."

I had tried so hard to pretend I hadn't heard that earlier. It was easier to blame the person who was blackmailing me than to question his real motives. I just couldn't picture the great Aiden Campbell needing to report to anyone but himself. He was unapologetic in everything he did.

"Who are you answering to, Aiden?"

"Let's just say that I owed some cars to some dangerous women and leave it at that," he replied. His shoulders drew back to their earlier tense position and his eyes were dark again, stopping me from pushing any further. Whatever Aiden was caught up in was bigger than I imagined.

"I'm sorry," I said, brushing my hand out to touch his. I wasn't sure exactly what I was apologising for. I didn't know if I was sorry for shouting, sorry for blaming him or just sorry about the entire mess. All I did know was that we weren't going to accomplish anything if I kept blowing up at him. I wasn't about to forgive him just yet though. Obviously, Aiden still expected me to work with him to get me out of bed at such a ridiculous time. For now, I was going to suffocate my pride and satisfy whatever need he had for me.

"It's okay." He gave my hand a quick squeeze and started the car, driving out of my street.

"So, where to now?" I asked, shifting back to sit properly in my seat.

Aiden tightened his grip on the steering wheel and took a moment before replying. "Sasha didn't come home last night and I haven't heard from her since the heist," he replied. "We're going to go find her."

We were going back to where the entire mess started. We were going back to Fairview Drive.

* * *

As Aiden parked the Lancer just around the corner from where I last saw Brooke, I took a second to breathe. I wasn't ready for this. I wasn't ready for the ride with Aiden to be over, either. We hadn't spoken a word to each other the whole time, but somehow the massive load of crap he had to deal with just now made him less guarded with me. I felt like I could see a real person under the ruthless persona.

Reluctantly, I released my hand from Aiden's grip. I had only touched his nervously drumming fingers to calm him down, because he was making me more nervous too. The firm pressure he responded with was so reassuring I didn't want to pull away. But now wasn't the time to be thinking about my feelings for him.

With my head pounding from the exertion of crying all night, I focused on the few streets within the industrial area. They were lined with nothing except warehouses and old abandoned business buildings.

Last night, the warehouse windows looked eerie, as if they could drown us in their darkness. Now, in the daylight, the buildings on Fairview Drive looked empty and dull, with only a layer of dust keeping us from peering straight inside them.

"Let's be quick," Aiden said quietly, stepping out of the vehicle and taking hold of my hand once more without hesitation. "We'll check what's happening and then go, okay?"

I nodded hesitantly and tried to gulp with my dry mouth. Brooke was going to be here and I wasn't ready. I had never seen a dead body before. I breathed in deeply and closed my eyes to calm my nerves.

"We don't have to do this, you know?" he said, squeezing my hand lightly. "You can go home and I can look for Sasha myself."

"No, I'm okay. We've come this far already."

Aiden let go of my hand and walked around the corner. I shuffled two paces behind him, watching his reaction to avoid looking at the actual scene. When his body went rigid, I unwillingly looked up.

There was no body, no blood, no nothing.

For a moment I thought it was all a mistake. Maybe Brooke was okay; maybe she'd got home on her own. Then my guts contracted with the image of the pool of blood in front of my feet. No way had she got herself out of here, dead or alive.

Who were we messing with? No way would an amateur take a body and risk being caught with it. Whoever did this wasn't afraid to kill and dispose of another person. That had to be the most terrifying thing I could ever imagine.

"Who the hell owned those cars?" I could feel the start of a paralysing panic attack coming along just as Aiden clamped his hand over my mouth and pulled me closer to him.

"Shh!" He pointed in front of us. "Someone's here."

Closing my eyes and matching my breaths to the beat of his

heart, I calmed myself enough to look in the direction he was pointing to. Three men came barrelling towards us with a glint of metal in their hands. So much for calming down; my breathing hitched at the realisation that they were holding guns.

"Stay quiet and let me deal with this," Aiden whispered into my ear. I could feel my heartbeat pounding against my ribs. "If we run they'll shoot us, okay?"

No more shooting, please no more shooting. I nodded my head and turned my attention back to the approaching men.

The closer they got, the more my muscles protested. The man standing between the two muscular ones was very attractive, which terrified me even more. He was a foot or so shorter than the other two, with a smooth baby-like face—he couldn't be any older than 40, even though he carried himself with a confidence belonging to someone much older. He wore a midnight blue suit that screamed wealth and his face was void of emotion. The two men on either side of him wore sour expressions and their broad shoulders hunched slightly. Their suits looked cheap and their skin was littered with scars and bruises.

The man in the middle gestured for the other two to quicken their pace and when he caught my eyes, everything suddenly went cold, as if someone had sucked the warmth out of the air.

I recognised this man.

The same face had plagued the prime time news channels for as long as I had been old enough to tolerate them. The very same face that was linked to murder, drugs and violence. I was looking into the eyes of Australia's notoriously ruthless Mob boss, Bobby Zangari.

"Come back for more did ya, you little shit?" the tougher looking henchman said.

I stared up at him and saw his crooked stained teeth flash beneath his snarl.

"Calm down, Tommy," Bobby said in a sickly sweet tone. If

it weren't for the fact that they were holding guns and obviously had no trouble firing them, I might have believed he meant us no harm. "You will treat our friends with respect."

Friends? I don't think I'd like to be friends with the Zangari family.

He walked closer to me and I felt Aiden's grip tighten around my arm. I instinctively leaned closer into him.

"Where are my manners?" the Mob boss said, holding out his hand. I gingerly placed my hand in his, which he pulled to his lips and kissed. "The name's Bobby and those are my brothers, Tommy and Frank."

I was only barely able to resist flinching. I just hoped he didn't notice the trembling. I was so scared, and even with Aiden right beside me I had never felt as entirely helpless as I did in that moment.

"Boss." Tommy's rough voice made him sound a lot older than he appeared to be. "There were more than just these two."

"So it would seem," Bobby mused, giving us a quick look up and down. "Where are the others?"

I stiffened when Aiden let go of my hand. We couldn't name the others, everyone knew that. Okay, so maybe that was more to do with the police. However, the only knowledge I had about Bobby and the Mob were some Crime Stopper advertisements and news reports, so I doubt letting him know exactly who stole his cars was a smart thing to do.

"I don't know what you mean," Aiden replied coolly.

Tommy cocked his gun and stormed up to hold it against Aiden's forehead.

A yelp slipped from my mouth before I could stop it. It's not like you could blame me; Tommy was holding a damn gun to Aiden's head and Bobby wasn't even moving to intervene or anything. Everything was just so out of control that it felt like any minute we were going to break through the thin film of normalcy. My heart was running a marathon and everything inside me screamed to run and curl up in a hole far away.

"That's enough, Tommy. Perhaps he has forgotten about last night? Let me refresh your memory, boy," he said. "Last night, you and your lady friend here, along with five others, disrespected my men and me by coming into our neighbourhood and stealing two of our Porsches."

All I could do was stare back at Bobby in complete disbelief. The realisation that we had stolen from the Mob dawned on me with a painful clench of my stomach. If I had the ability to get angry at that moment, I would have yelled at Aiden for keeping this from me. Stealing cars was one thing but stealing from the Mob was something completely beyond my comprehension.

I was going to be sick. I think it was safe to say that we had royally messed up—colossally. All I could do was wrap my arms around my stomach and hold myself together as if I was a roll of thread threatening to unravel.

I had to talk to Bobby and make this right. I needed to explain myself. "Look, Bobby, I'm sorry. We didn't know they were your cars, honestly. We would never disrespect you—"

Smack. I heard the slap before I felt it. Frank had walked straight up to me and hit me hard enough that my cheek instantly went numb. I guess I should have been grateful for that because as soon as the initial shock wore off, I had to clench my teeth together to stop from whimpering.

Oh god, that hurt. Tears formed in my eyes and the taste of blood filled my mouth. I stumbled backwards in my urgency to put as much distance between Frank and me as possible.

Aiden lunged forward and grabbed him by the collar. All I could focus on was the painful throb that started to spread across my right cheek.

"You will not speak to Bobby, you pathetic little girl," Frank said, raising his hand again.

"You don't touch her!" Aiden shouted, then he punched him in the nose.

The pure rage in Aiden's voice made me instantly forget my cheek. His eyes had darkened with a possessive anger that terrified me.

"Enough!" Bobby called out in annoyance.

I held my breath and silently willed Aiden to control his anger. Just when I thought I was about to witness a full-on brawl, Aiden slowly removed his hands from Frank's collar and returned to his spot next to me. He placed a gentle hand on my cheek, which was now burning, and looked intently at me. All I could muster was a weak smile to let him know I was okay, but it must've been enough because he turned back to Bobby and slid his hand onto the small of my back.

What surprised me was Bobby. He gripped Frank's hand in a death grip and yanked him away from us.

"You will never lay a hand on a woman again, do you hear me?" he said with a voice full of aggression. "If I hear you so much as raise your tone with a woman like that again, so help me, I will have you six feet under before the day is through. Do you understand me?"

I hadn't expected that. Then again, I hadn't expected this entire day to turn out as it had.

Frank's expression was hard to work out. He was trapped between obedience and disgust, clenching his jaw and falling back in line with Tommy. "Yes, boss."

He reminded me a little of a dog. He was loyal to his owner even if he didn't agree with his orders. I just hoped Bobby's orders stayed along the lines of "don't hit women" and didn't change to "kill them both".

"We truly are sorry, sir," I continued, ignoring the sting in my cheek. "If we had known they were your cars we wouldn't have taken them. We meant you no disrespect."

Bobby kept staring at Aiden and me with a mix of suspicion and amusement, as if he was trying to decide whether to congratulate or crucify us. I'd give anything for it to be the former. I didn't want to see what he would do if he deemed us an enemy.

"Whose idea was it to do a slow start, as well as use tinfoil to cut the alarm?"

Hang on, how could he have known about that? It was a spur of the moment decision.

"The foil was Nicole's idea," he said. "It was my idea to do the slow start so the engine wouldn't be too loud starting up."

"Impressive," Bobby mused.

Why would he tell him that? Aiden must have had some kind of death wish and now he was taking me down in a twisted suicide pact that I hadn't agreed to.

Bobby relaxed his stance and gestured for his goons to lower their guns. "You're lucky I'm feeling generous today so I'll let your girlfriend keep her life." He smiled wickedly at me. "I do, however, expect you to return my vehicles in perfect condition by midnight tomorrow or I won't be so forgiving. And don't even think about going to the cops, young lady. I'll know, and that will be very, very bad for you."

Wait, what? Bobby was giving us a chance when he had killed for less? Not even kidding, he actually broke two of a man's fingers for accidentally bumping into him when he was visiting a family member in prison. Bobby was not a forgiving man.

Regardless, I wasn't about to argue. I swallowed dryly and nodded my head. Thankfully that was enough confirmation for him. I wasn't foolish enough to argue with him when he was doing something that seemed so out of character. He was giving us a chance to fix everything.

His eyes flicked to Aiden and that's when my brain caught up with what else Bobby had said. He knew Aiden's name.

Aiden might be extremely popular in Silverlake, but I didn't think that extended to the underworld.

I desperately wanted to ask how Bobby knew him and why he was being lenient, but I bit my tongue. It wasn't that hard since I could feel Frank and Tommy eyeing me with disgust. I needed to run, cry, or just do something. I couldn't be here anymore.

As if he sensed my fear, Aiden strengthened his grip on my lower back and steered me towards his car.

Just as we turned to leave, another question entered my mind. I couldn't let the fear that had a vice-like grip on my heart keep me from spinning back around and locking eyes with Bobby.

"Wait," I said before I had a chance to stop myself. I kept my voice as professional and cool as possible. "If it's okay with you, sir, I would like to know one more thing."

He eyed me briefly before nodding his head. "All right."

"What about Brooke? Where is she? Is she alive? Did the cops find her?"

"My, aren't we an inquisitive one?" He laughed smoothly. "I'm starting to like you. As for your friend, I wouldn't be too concerned. We have taken care of her. If you know what's best for you, you'll leave it alone."

Even with the vague explanation, his tone was clear enough. Brooke was dead and if we didn't want to end up the same way, we had better forget everything we saw. I wasn't about to test out his threat.

With a quick nod, I allowed Aiden to snake a possessive arm around my waist and guide me away.

"Midnight tomorrow or your lives," Bobby said, pocketing his gun. "Oh, and please tell Sasha that she has something of ours."

He knew Sasha as well? This was crazy. I must have smacked my head on my bedhead last night or something. This type of stuff just didn't happen to girls like me.

Bobby waved us off and walked back in the direction he came from, followed by his brothers.

We stayed quiet on our way back to the car. Aiden's hand didn't leave my waist until I was safely seated in the Lancer.

It had to be almost half past seven and people would be just starting to wake up now to start their day. Libby would be slamming her hand against the alarm clock in an attempt to silence it. It wouldn't take her long to discover that I wasn't there and I wasn't looking forward to having to explain all this.

I quickly pulled my phone out and switched it off. The last thing I wanted to do was tell her this over the phone. That conversation would have to wait until I was safely back in my bed and had an icepack on my face.

"Are you okay?" Aiden said, startling me.

I looked at him, trying to make sense of his expression. His eyes were still black and his usual honey coloured irises were now lifeless. His mouth was frozen in a tight line and his eyebrows knitted together in concentration.

"What?" I said dumbly after I realised I had been staring the whole time. Smooth, Nicole, real smooth.

"Are you okay?" he repeated. "Did Frank hurt you?"

I smiled as the colour returned to his eyes. I don't know what was happening with the two of us. I still resented him over everything and I couldn't just forget it all. However, I couldn't exactly explain why, but I was starting to warm up to him.

"No, I'm fine," I replied, touching my tender cheek. "I'm just confused."

"What about?"

"About why you didn't tell me that we were stealing from the Mob," I replied, anger slowly seeping into my voice. "Surely you must've known how stupid that would be?"

He narrowed his eyes at me and shifted in his seat. "I didn't say anything to you because I didn't know," he quipped. "Sasha found the cars. She told me they belonged to a group of rich kids with too much time on their hands. I don't know why she would lie to me."

"That's another thing," I pressed on. "What did he want with Sasha? What does she have of his?"

"I don't know, okay!"

Wow, okay. I shut my mouth and stared at him. He sighed and ran a hand through his curls. I had never seen him so dishevelled before. He had always been perfectly put together.

"I'm sorry," I said, reaching for his hand.

He threaded our fingers together and looked back up at me. "I don't know what's going on and I won't until I talk to Sasha," he said. "All I do know is that we have to get those cars back before we run out of time."

Aiden gave my hand one last squeeze before letting go and starting the engine. I barely had time to get my seatbelt on before we were tearing down the street.

"Why do you think he let us go?" I asked. The question had been on my mind since we left the warehouse.

"I'm sure he has his reasons."

"What do you mean?"

"Stop worrying, Edwards," he said as he drifted around a corner. "It's probably best we don't question it."

I nodded absentmindedly. There were so many unanswered questions that my head was starting to spin. Suddenly, things had become more complicated than I had ever thought possible. I felt sick in my stomach whenever I thought about how close we'd come to ending up like Brooke. Bobby was planning something, I just knew it. He never let anyone go—especially not those who dared to steal from him. He also knew Sasha, which was the most puzzling thing of all. When I really thought about it, I realised I didn't actually know anything about her. She was much colder than her brother, that's for sure.

To be honest she scared me, although not as much as Bobby did. I shuddered as his threat ran through my head. He wasn't kidding when he said we'd regret it. He wouldn't hesitate to kill us.

I couldn't be a scared little girl anymore though. I wouldn't be able to switch off the fear that was pumping through my veins like oxygen. However, I could bury it far enough inside that I would be able to focus on holding up our end of the deal. If we wanted to live long enough to see graduation, we needed to get those cars back.

"So where to now?" I asked, curious about exactly what he had done with the cars and praying that they were in one piece. Aiden could have taken them to the moon for all I knew.

"We're off to the other side of town to pay an old friend a visit," he replied, pushing his foot harder on the accelerator.

Time was something we couldn't afford to waste right now.

10
The Girls

The warehouse was the strangest place I had ever seen. From the outside it looked like a dingy broken-down factory that needed to be boarded up or knocked down. A thick layer of mud disguised the faded red of the building. The glass windows had cracks stretching across them until they joined in an almost spider web design. You would think the place would be condemned, if it weren't for the smoke coming from the massive chimney poking out the roof.

The inside of the building, however, had undergone a remarkable transformation. The walls were jammed with tools and pictures of stripped down and modified cars. The floors were mostly clean except for the half-faded grease stains. The sound of a drill blended in with the classic rock that blared from the speakers positioned throughout the whole warehouse.

Aiden walked towards the upstairs office. As I followed him I looked at the mechanics, who were busy changing oil and rebuilding engines. A few of them looked our way and smiled, waving at Aiden. Once we had crossed the entire length of the room I realised why the shop was so neat and unlike other car repair shops I had seen before. It was because every single mechanic I could see in the building was female.

"Pretty unique, huh?" Aiden smirked after catching me staring at them. "Dom says she hires the women that other shops won't take. Apparently sexism is still an issue."

"Dom?"

"She's the owner and the person we're here to see," Aiden

replied. "Her name is Dominique, but everyone just calls her Dom. She's a bit of a hard arse."

I swallowed nervously as we entered the reception area. If Dom had the Porsches then this wasn't going to be easy. Selling stolen cars was one thing but asking for them back was another matter entirely.

I was so caught up in my thoughts that it took me a moment to realise just how different the reception area was to the rest of the place. The entire space was feminine and looked like it was right out of an episode of *Gossip Girl*. The walls were a lilac colour and were complimented by plush white carpet that still had that freshly cleaned smell. Nailed to the wall were dozens of signed pictures of celebrities, thanking them for their services.

Iggy Azalea boasted about her "rock star worthy" tune up and Liam Hemsworth thanked them for seeing him on such short notice. I didn't even know people like that visited Silverlake, unless Dom had previously been set up somewhere else.

"Aiden!" A petite woman in high heels rushed from behind her desk to greet us.

"Hey, Tess," he replied smoothly.

A strong wave of jealousy washed over me as she went to hug him. I mentally shook myself for even thinking like that. Aiden was free to touch whomever he wanted and it was none of my business.

Who was I trying to fool? Of course I was jealous. The very idea that Aiden touched anyone like he touched me made my skin crawl. There was no point lying to myself about that. As much as I hated to admit it, I was attracted to him. I just didn't understand it though. Aiden made me so angry all the time, but then he'd pull a Jekyll and Hyde, dropping his guard and replacing my anger with this fluttery light feeling.

Oh crap, I was crushing on Aiden and Tess was seriously pissing me off. Nobody hugged another person for that long, thank you very much. I cleared my throat to draw their attention.

"Oh, sorry." Tess walked over and held out her hand. I eyed it for a moment before sighing and shaking it. "Welcome to Dom's Used Car Dealership. What can I do for you two?"

"We were hoping to see Dom, if she's free?" Aiden asked.

I removed my hand from Tess's hastily and crossed them against my chest.

"One second, I'll check for you," she beamed, swaying back to her desk.

God, could she be any more obvious? Seriously, it was pathetic. There was no way Aiden would ever go for someone like her. She was a complete airhead and flipped her hair way too often to be normal.

I felt a slight nudge to my shoulder and I looked over to see Aiden staring at me with a knowing glance.

"Shut up."

"You've got nothing to worry about, baby," he replied with his usual smirk before running his eyes down my body. "I'm not going anywhere."

Yep, there was the Aiden I knew well. Giving him my best eye roll, I returned my focus to Malibu Barbie. She pressed the buzzer on her intercom and asked if Dom was free to see any-one. She must've gotten a yes because she then pushed herself back on to her feet and flicked her strawberry blonde hair out of her face.

"Follow me please," she said, glancing at us as she walked through the back hallway to a small office door that had a thick steel handle. "Good luck."

* * *

Dom's office was also surprising: the walls were a dark red with a main feature wall painted in a black charcoal colour. Pictures filled with smiling faces covered the wall. One particular photo showed Dom with her arms wrapped lovingly around a gorgeous brunette woman. However, the woman standing in front of us didn't resemble the one in all the photos. She wore tight leather pants and a tank top, which only caused her sour expression to stand out more.

"Well?" she said unpleasantly. "Come in and sit down."

Aiden brushed past me, lightly touching my back before sitting down on the leather couch in the middle of the office. I quietly followed him and sat down with our knees touching. The comforting gesture was something I needed more than I would care to admit.

"Dom, you're looking lovely as usual," Aiden said slyly, giving her a cheeky smile.

She stood in front of us with her hands on her hips. Her tall frame was intimidating. Her black hair was cut in sharp angles and her fringe framed her electric blue eyes.

"Cut the shit, Aiden," she said impatiently. "Explain why you're disrupting me after I made it clear you were never to do so."

"We need the Porsches back."

With a humourless laugh, she slid her hands from her hips to fold around her chest. "You must be joking. There's no way you'd come in here and ask that of me."

"I think I just did." Aiden's jaw had tightened and a faint tint of red spread across his face. He needed to cool it before he really pissed off this woman. I bumped my knee against his as some form of comfort, but his anger remained etched in his features.

"Excuse me?" Dom retorted, rage seeping into her voice.

"Look, Dom, we need the Porsches back because they don't belong to us," I said in an attempt to diffuse the situation.

"Well, of course they don't belong to you, they're stolen," she replied, shifting her cold gaze onto me. "Who are you, anyway?"

"Her name is Nicole and she's right," Aiden chimed in a little more calmly. "Those cars belong to Bobby Zangari."

The little colour that was in Dom's face drained and her eyes widened. "You stole from the Zangari family!" she yelled. "Do you have a death wish?"

Okay, now she had a right to be angry. We did make the mistake of stealing from the worst possible people, and we'd dragged her into it.

"Of course not," Aiden said, standing up. "That's why we need those cars back."

"How did you even get into this mess?" she asked, completely disregarding what Aiden had said. "Were you that desperate to get rid of me?"

Whoa, hang on a second. Was there more to this relationship than just cars? Aiden's stance hadn't changed and he didn't look confused so he clearly knew what she meant, even if I didn't.

"I didn't knowingly do this, I'm not stupid," he argued. "I didn't know they belonged to Bobby until a few hours ago when I ran into him."

Dom simply raised an eyebrow suspiciously.

Aiden had made a valid point earlier. Dom was a hard arse, and he wasn't going to get anywhere if he continued to antagonise her. Remembering the pep talk I gave myself after our run in with Bobby, I spoke up before I could talk myself out of it.

"Dom, please, we need those cars back or Bobby is going to come for us. He's already killed our friend."

Both faces swung towards me as I sat up straighter on the couch. Holding my hands tighter together, I prayed that she would be generous.

"Why should I help you?"

"Because who do you think Bobby will come for next when he's done with us?" Aiden replied.

She had to know he was right. Bobby was definitely not the type to give up on what he wanted, and if we couldn't return the cars then he wouldn't hesitate to come looking for them.

Several minutes passed without a single word uttered. Neither of us knew what Dom's decision would be. Just when I thought she had gone mute, Dom sighed loudly and rubbed her forehead in frustration.

"I guess I don't really have a choice in the matter," she said. "You can have the cars back."

Well, that was easier than I thought it would be. I smiled at Aiden as Dom turned toward her polished desk, but I faltered when I noticed his sour expression. Typical Aiden. He wouldn't even be grateful that she was helping us out.

"Thank you, Dom," I answered for the both of us, hoping to keep everything peaceful. "We're sorry about the mishap."

I waited for Aiden to get up, but he remained seated in an intense staring match with Dom. It was painfully obvious that he didn't like her. I just wish I knew why.

Eventually, Aiden rose from his seat and stomped towards the door. He had just reached out to open it when Dom cleared her throat loudly.

"And where do you think you're going?"

"To the garage," Aiden spat. "That would be where you store the Porsches."

"Yes, you'd know that, wouldn't you?" she said with a smirk. I didn't like where this was going. She was too content for someone who was losing two expensive cars. "But I'm not just going to give them to you, am I? It's going to cost you."

"I knew there would be a catch." He spun around and stalked back to face her. "There always is with you."

"Well, you know me," she teased. "I never like to disappoint." Dom slipped her hand beneath her top and pulled out a thin silver chain. Attached to it was a small silver key.

She unclasped the necklace and slotted the key into her desk drawer. "You see, giving you back those cars means I'm going to be out $200,000," she said, rummaging in the drawer and pulling out a piece of yellow lined paper. "You're going to have to replace that cash."

I quickly stepped in when Aiden looked like he was about to protest. We'd been lucky so far; I didn't want it to run out. "What do you want us to do?"

She switched her gaze from where it was glued to Aiden onto me. With a smirk, she slid the paper cross the table. "I have other clients who need to be taken care of." She folded her arms and smiled smugly. "This is a list of the types of cars that have the parts I need for my clients."

"How many are you expecting us to get?" Aiden snapped.

Dom observed us for a moment before replying. "Nine. And I want them all here by tomorrow night."

"Nine?" Aiden raised his voice in disbelief. "How do you expect us to get ten cars that fast?"

"That's not my problem, is it?" she replied icily. "Now do we have a deal or do I need to get Tess to show you out?"

"Wait … So if we get you ten cars from this list then you'll return the Porsches to us in perfect condition?" I questioned, wanting her to confirm it.

"That's what I said, princess."

I hated being called princess. It reminded me of the prima donna girls from Sterling High, who spent their class time painting their nails and talking about the latest guy they wanted to see shirtless. I was not a princess.

Huffing at the term, I turned to Aiden to see what he thought. He gave me a slight nod and a half smile before linking his fingers through mine.

"Guess it's a deal then," I replied sarcastically, snatching up the list and tugging Aiden towards the exit.

"So kitty does have claws? How sweet," Dom called out from where she was sitting behind her desk. "Oh and Aiden, we're no longer even."

Aiden tensed and gripped my hand a little too tightly. His eyes faded into the black that only meant one thing: danger.

"What?"

"You heard me. The deal was for three Porsches. You broke it, so you still owe me."

The room went silent; all I could hear was my heartbeat and Aiden's laboured breath. Heat was radiating off him and anger flooded his eyes. I swiped my finger against the inside of his palm and he inhaled deeply.

Without answering her, Aiden pulled me out of the room and through the shop. A few of the mechanics turned our way, but Aiden didn't stop until we were back outside.

"What was that about?"

"Dom and I have history." He tried to pass it off as nothing except his body betrayed him. He was still tense and his hand still clenched tightly around mine. "Come on, we'll talk in the car. We have to get you home before anyone realises you're missing."

He released my hand and climbed into the driver's seat. I didn't know what we were going to do now. We had just over thirty-six hours to steal ten cars and get them to Dom so we could get the Porsches back and return them to Bobby by midnight tomorrow. It was so impossible I couldn't even stress about it properly. A little part of my brain was panicking, but the rest of it just refused to accept the situation as real.

I was still clutching the sheet of paper that Dom had handed us. Without looking at it, I pocketed the list and sat in the passenger's seat once more. There was so much I didn't know. Aiden's history with Dom had to be messed up if they couldn't be in a room together without tempers flying. I wanted to know how Aiden knew her and why he needed to steal Porsches to be even. What did they need to be even for?

Aiden backed the car out and I finally unclenched my hands. The tension was still etched deeply in his face but I couldn't stop myself from wondering what had happened to him, especially not now. Aiden and I were in this together and if we were going to make it out in one piece, we were going to have to trust each other.

It was time to share everything.

11
Decisions

Aiden was so unnaturally quiet on the drive to my place that it was starting to give me the creeps. He still had the same darkness in his eyes, and although he was calmer than he was with Dom, he was still tense.

I tried to stay silent, I really did, but what he said about his history with Dom and his reaction to her was confusing. I could only think of one reason for their explosive emotions.

"Were you and Dom together?" I blurted out. Aiden looked at me questioningly. "You mentioned you two have history." I expected something along the lines of confusion or annoyance; I didn't expect Aiden to start laughing.

"Dom doesn't swing that way," he said with a smirk. "I've just known her since I was fourteen."

"Known her how?"

It probably wasn't the smartest choice to push him. He screwed up his face the moment I asked. Aiden gripped the steering wheel so tightly his knuckles turned white. It reminded me of how he acted when we went to find Sasha and he held onto the steering wheel so tightly that he left an indent. I did the only thing I could think of to keep him grounded, placing my hand on his leg in comfort.

Wow, okay. I was touching Aiden. This was not like me at all.

His grip on the wheel relaxed and with a heavy exhale, he glanced my way. "As you know, Dom deals with stolen cars," he said, changing lanes. "When I was younger I started stealing and selling them to her for cash."

"Why?" I asked. Stealing cars for cash didn't sound like a whole lot of fun.

"I wasn't prepared to enter the family business and I needed my own money." If Aiden was aware of how weird this sounded, he didn't show it. He kept his eyes focused on the road but he seemed to be staring beyond it. "My cousin runs a drug ring that accepts stolen cars as currency so they taught me everything. I found out about Dom's operation after I raided my dad's file of potential clients. Of course, I removed it so he wouldn't approach her."

This was the first time I had ever heard Aiden talk about his dad. I couldn't blame him. I didn't know what type of guy his dad was, but if Aiden chose to work for Dom instead of him then he had to be bad.

"It was good for a while, but when I wanted out a year ago, Dom said our debt wasn't settled."

"Your debt?"

"Dom helped me out of a difficult situation. If it wasn't for her I would be stuck working for my dad. Trust me, that's bad. She paid me for the cars, but she also gave me the opportunity to be my own man. As far as she's concerned, that gives her a claim over me."

Squeezing his leg reassuringly, I finally gave myself the chance to really look at him properly. Aiden's mysterious reputation was starting to slowly unravel layer by layer and I wasn't sure what I was supposed to think anymore. Aiden was like a magnet for all things nasty and it seemed like he owned it with pride. Except, maybe this time he didn't.

"Is that what you meant when you told me that everyone has to answer to someone?"

He nodded and shifted gears. "The Porsches were supposed to be the end," he said. "It was Sasha's idea. Dom wouldn't be able to resist them and it would be enough to get her to let me go."

Hearing Aiden talk about someone else having power over him was weird. He was always the one in control. No one messed with him and even the teachers at Sterling High didn't care enough to intervene when he walked in ten minutes before class ended or took a phone call during the lesson.

The mention of Sasha made me tense up a little. She was linked with everything to do with the heist and that set off alarm bells in my head. Bobby knew her and Aiden said it was her idea to begin with. I didn't know what to make of it, but there was something I did know.

She couldn't be trusted. Not even a little bit.

"Why don't you just tell Dom to piss off?"

"Because despite her appearance, she's very dangerous," he said. "She is very protective of her girls and her operation. If you threaten that, she can be just as dangerous as Bobby."

My throat tightened, making it hard to breathe. We had two ruthless people expecting us to deliver cars to them. Once again I thought frantically about how I got into this situation, and how I could get out. I was pretty sure that Aiden wouldn't really carry out his threat about putting cheating on my record after all we'd been through—at least, I didn't think so, although who knew with Aiden?

But that was pretty irrelevant now, wasn't it? Bobby Zangari knew my name. He could probably find out where I lived. And he knew that I had helped to steal his precious Porsches. He would happily kill me and maybe even my family, and I had no chance of hiding from him in this tiny town. My only chance of getting my life back, however slim, was to go along with this *Grand Theft Auto* scenario and pray we could pull it off.

"I guess we'd better do a good job," I said flatly. What else was there to say? I was far from ready to do this, but there was no other way.

I might as well say goodbye to Murdoch, because even if

we managed to pull this off I was still going to be a thief with Brooke's death on my conscience and her blood permanently absorbed into my skin.

Aiden looked at me with the same expression he had when he noticed the tear stains on my face this morning. I hated that expression.

"What?" I said edgily.

"You seem different."

I'm sure I did since I didn't exactly feel like the Nic I usually was. "Good different or bad different?"

He smiled at me and placed his hand over the one I had resting on his leg. "Neither," he replied. "You're just not the same girl who got flustered when I caught her stealing DVDs."

Yeah, I guess he was right. The Nic who stole those DVDs and the Nic of today were entirely separate. My mood swings were so extreme it was like there were six different emotions battling to take over. I just didn't know what to do anymore. This wasn't supposed to be my life and the only person who really understood it was Aiden. I should hate him for dragging me into this but I couldn't seem to do it.

He was a lot like my mirror. He reflected the same ambition that coursed through me. His ambition wasn't aimed at the things mine were, but it was just as strong and that was why I couldn't seem to walk away.

"I guess I'm just tired of being afraid." Okay, so maybe I wasn't going to just switch my fear off that easily, but wallowing wasn't going to help. "Besides, if you could handle this world for three years then I can handle it for another night."

"It wasn't all that bad, really."

I bit my lip and removed my hand from his lap before sitting up slightly. "Oh I'm sure," I replied in my best attempt at a disinterested tone. "You were quite popular with Tess."

Oh wow, that sounded crazy. I really needed to get some

sleep before these mood swings became a permanent thing. I couldn't even look at him because I knew how ridiculous I sounded, but it was like my brain was disconnected from my mouth. I had no control over it.

He chuckled and lowered his voice until it was almost a growl. "Your jealousy is adorable," he said, taking hold of my hand once more. I was going to protest and make it clear that I was not jealous, thank you very much, but then he raised my hand to his lips and placed a chaste kiss to it. It was warm where his lips were pressed and it tingled lightly. "I think you're adorable."

I ducked my head to keep Aiden from seeing me blush for the rest of the trip. He would never let me live it down if he saw. Blushing like a little fan girl was not something I did and this was just embarrassing. Besides, I really shouldn't have read too much into it anyway. Aiden was a flirt and everyone knew that.

Yeah, we may have become closer this past weekend, but that didn't mean that we wouldn't go back to hating each other just as quickly when this was all over.

* * *

We pulled up in front of my house with a few minutes to spare. My parents were supposed to be waking up soon for work, so if I wanted to stay punishment free, I needed to start moving.

I opened the door just as Aiden cut the engine.

"Wait." He stilled my movements with his hand and I turned in my seat until we were facing each other. "We'll need to get together tonight to discuss our next move. We need to figure out how we are going to get all these cars in time."

Staring towards the house for a moment, I contemplated our next crazy adventure. I was stupid to think it would be as easy as telling everyone we were sorry. What was even worse was that I thought our theft at the Bellvale Mall was as bad as it could get.

"What about the others?" I asked, stepping out of the car and turning to shut the door.

Aiden hadn't mentioned the others all morning and honestly, it was strange that they didn't come with him. I would've thought they'd want to know what happened, especially Greg.

"They don't know about any of this. I know what happened to Brooke messed you up so I wanted to take you to see her."

I'm sure that was supposed to be a considerate thought, but it just made my stomach churn. I wanted to argue that he was so beyond wrong with that, but in the end it was exactly what I needed.

I wasn't normal. What normal person wanted to check that someone was really dead? Aiden was the only one who really understood me right now, and that scared the shit out of me.

"Thank you."

With a small smile, he started the engine and let it idle. "We'll need them in on this though; it's too much for just the two of us."

I hadn't even considered the possibility of us doing it on our own.

"Why don't you speak to Libby now and text me what she says? I'll speak to the others and let you know what's happening later tonight. Will you be able to sneak out after dark?"

"Yeah, it should be fine," I said with a slight smile. This had been the longest morning of my life and all I wanted to do was curl up into my bed and sleep. Except, with all this drama going on, I couldn't see that happening.

Aiden nodded and drove out of the driveway, disappearing around the corner.

With him gone, a million thoughts popped up to assault my brain. We were so in over our heads that I couldn't be sure we weren't going to end up like Brooke. I didn't know her that well, but her death still made my insides hurt. We couldn't dwell on what happened if we wanted to get through this, but I couldn't stop my mind from wandering to everything that I was going to miss out on.

And I definitely couldn't help it when my thoughts turned to the fact that I still hadn't been kissed. It was silly, I knew that. I just couldn't help it. If this entire thing blew up in our faces then I was going to die as a sixteen-year-old, never-been-kissed, pathetic dork.

My mind flicked to Aiden and his golden eyes. The one guy I couldn't stand was the one guy who understood me most. Things were different now though. We were like magnets trying to stay apart; it was inevitable that we would connect.

I took a deep breath and made my way to the front door. I could spend all day thinking about the things I'd never get to do, but it would be pointless. I needed to get myself together before my lack of concentration got us killed.

I slowly turned the key in the front door and quietly stepped in. As silently as I could, I tiptoed across the hall and into the lounge room. If my parents caught me they would jump to conclusions and assume I had been out all night. My parents were amazing people, but they were always cautious. They made it clear that I had to be home before it was dark outside or I'd be subjected to a long boring lecture about the dangerous people lurking in the dark.

I never thought they'd be right.

I spent so much time doubting them and just dismissing their warnings as parents being parents that I never really thought about the real lesson they were trying to teach me. They wanted me to be careful of the darkness within people. What would they say if they saw me now?

I was so preoccupied with my thoughts that I almost tripped on the coffee table, saving myself in the last second.

"Nic." I heard a harsh whisper come from the top of the stairs. I swallowed quickly and stared up to where I was convinced my mum was standing. "Where have you been?"

"Libs?" I whispered back, recognising her fluffy pink slippers.

"Don't Libs me. Where have you been?" she repeated more aggressively. "I tried calling you five times in the past hour and I was sent straight to voicemail. You had me worried sick."

"Would you chill out? I'm fine, aren't I?" I snapped. "Besides, we have bigger problems than that."

I walked upstairs and pulled Libby into her bedroom. With a deep breath, I filled her in on Bobby Zangari and his threat, as well as Dom and the deal we made with her. Libby didn't move the entire time. I could see her processing everything, and if the situation wasn't so bad I would have laughed at her instant change in expression. Her features contorted into fear when she finally understood what I had said.

"So you're telling me that you and Aiden actually went up against Bobby Zangari?" she asked incredulously. "Where was my invite?"

"Seriously, that's what you're upset about?"

"Yeah," she replied with a shrug. "Just feels like we aren't in this together anymore."

"Don't be ridiculous. Of course we are," I said, waving my hand dismissively. "Do you understand why we need to do this car heist for Dom? If we don't we might as well kiss our lives goodbye." My voice cracked slightly, betraying the tears I was trying so hard to keep from slipping. I was tired of the tears and I was tired of being the victim.

"So what are we going to do?" Libby said, brushing her arm against mine in comfort.

"Well, I spoke to Aiden and he wants to see all of us tonight, I'm guessing at Sasha's," I said, pulling my mobile phone from my pocket. "I better let him know that you're in."

"You and Aiden seem really close all of a sudden."

I could feel her eyes boring into the pocket where I'd returned my phone and I felt a little self-conscious. "I guess we are."

Libby bent down to replace her slippers with boots. "I'm going to school early. I'll meet you back here before we go to Sasha's," she said, moving to the table and picking up her keys. "Tell loverboy we'll be there to clean up the mess." She swiftly walked out the room, almost slamming the door shut as she left.

What the hell was that? I had no idea what was going on with her. She was all "team Aiden" when I didn't like him; however, now she seemed sour at the idea of the two of us. And she seemed to blame us for this mess when it was her idea to steal in the first place. I scowled in confusion. I just wanted my best friend back.

My phone beeped with a message from Aiden and I was so grateful for the distraction that I yanked it from my pocket and tapped open the message:

> **That's awesome Bonnie. The others are keen to meet. I'm going to pick you ladies up at 11ish. Don't miss me too much—Your Clyde x.**

Despite the situations with Dom and with Libby, I couldn't help smiling a little at the nicknames. Slipping my phone back into my pocket, I climbed the stairs to my bedroom. I felt exhausted, not only physically but mentally as well. There was no way I was going to be able to keep my eyes open long enough to sit through classes today and besides, missing one day of school wasn't the worst thing I had done recently.

Without changing, I fell into bed, determined to get some sleep before I had to face the others.

* * *

By the time Aiden was due to pick us up, Libby was back and still cold towards me. She continued to avoid my gaze while we grabbed our phones and the house keys, sneaking out the back door.

"What's your deal?" I didn't know why she was so distant with me and I couldn't fix it if she didn't tell me.

"Nothing," she said way too quickly. "Is Aiden meeting us here or are we walking?"

I wanted to talk about what was bothering her, but I could see Aiden flash his headlights from down the street.

"He's picking us up," I replied bluntly. If she wanted to give me the cold shoulder then fine. We didn't have time for this now anyway; we'd just have to deal with it later. "See him over there?"

I pointed out Aiden's Lancer and walked with Libby down the driveway and over to his car.

Just as we got within earshot she said, "So are you guys dating or what?"

I gaped at her and felt my cheeks go pink. Fortunately Aiden's windows were closed, so he didn't hear Libby's ill-timed question.

"Miss me already?" Aiden smirked as he pushed the door open for me.

"You wish," I replied, slipping in and waiting for Libby. She walked over with a sour face and pulled the back door open with a little more force than necessary.

"Hey, Libs," Aiden said as he turned the key in the ignition.

"Hi, handsome," she purred, suddenly all sweetness and light. Although not to me, I noticed. I might as well not have been there.

"Thanks for letting us hitch a ride to our life of crime. You're a corrupting influence, you know," she teased.

Aiden shot me a quick look, amused and quizzical, then slipped easily into his usual flirtatious routine with Libby. Whatever her problem was with me, it obviously wasn't big enough to make her drop the skank act with Aiden. If anything, she was more of a flirt than usual.

The night air whistled through the little crack in the window and I watched the lights from the surrounding houses dance across the front seat. I tried to keep my mind focused on the task ahead, I really did. I attempted to think of a plan to get what Dom wanted, but my thoughts kept slipping to why Libby was so upset with me.

I carefully listened as Libby kept up her constant chatter with Aiden. She leant across to his seat, her fingers drumming teasingly on his shoulder.

Then it finally became clear: Libby was jealous. She was the one who pushed us to take Aiden up on his deal, she was the one who got angry when Aiden and I were paired, and now we were close she was pissed.

I didn't fool myself that this was some sort of tragic love triangle. Sure, Aiden was hot, but if Libby had been into him she would have put a move on him before this. No, she had risked our lives and dragged me into this mess because she wanted what Aiden practically oozed—popularity.

How could I have missed that?

I glared at the side of her head, but she just ignored me and carried on teasing Aiden. I needed to talk to her or, better yet, to yell at her until I didn't feel so angry. I turned away and stared out the window, doing my best to forget she was there.

"You coming in, Nic?" Aiden asked, looking at me across from his seat.

I was so lost in my revelation that I hadn't realised that we had arrived and Libby had already gone inside. "Uh, yeah."

I fumbled with my seatbelt, finally unclipping it on the third attempt and pulling myself out of the car. Aiden was next to me the moment I closed the door.

"So tell me I didn't imagine the tension between Thelma and Louise?" I gave him a questioning look and he smirked. "You and Libs obviously."

"Your obsession with crime-committing couples is getting out of hand."

"And your skill at deflection is astounding," he quipped. "Now spill."

I sighed and rubbed my temple. I could feel a headache coming on. "It's a long and messy story," I replied. "Let's just drop it and focus on—oh, I don't know—not having an angry Mob boss and an insane car dealer on our backs."

He stared at me for a moment before nodding with a small smile. "There's something I think you should know before we go in though," he said suddenly. "Sasha's back."

"Seriously?"

He looked at me with pleading eyes. "She got scared so she ran," he explained. "She's not proud of it, but she can't take it back now."

Yeah whatever, we were all scared.

"So what did she take?"

"Sorry?"

"The thing Bobby mentioned? What does Sasha have of his?"

"Oh, nothing. It was just a misunderstanding."

Yeah, right. I opened my mouth to challenge the obvious lie, but his dark gold eyes were shut against me like Fort Knox.

I wasn't going to easily forget what happened and I certainly didn't trust Sasha, but there was so much going on that holding a grudge seemed kind of pointless. Being pissed at one person was exhausting enough.

12
What to do?

Sasha's house was darker than would be deemed necessary. The curtains hanging from the kitchen window were closed tightly, sealing off any light from the street lamps. The only available light in the room was coming from the crackling fireplace.

The others, who had all arrived before us, were occupying themselves while they waited.

Greg slumped on the couch, staring straight ahead as if he was watching some imaginary football game. Large purple bags hung below his deadened eyes and made him look years older than he actually was. Grief was carved on his face and my heart constricted at the reminder that Brooke wasn't with us anymore.

I wanted to comfort him and tell him that it was going to be okay. But that wasn't what he needed. Instead, I sat down next to him and lightly placed a hand on his briefly.

Of course he was upset. How could any of us be okay after what had happened?

What was unexpected, however, was Libby and Noah whispering harshly at each other. They were standing off to the side of the kitchen. Libby had her arms wrapped defensively around her chest while Noah was gesturing at her as if he were scolding a child.

I didn't know when they went from flirting to fighting but I guess there were a lot of things I was missing these days. She still refused to look anywhere near my direction, even when she turned away from Noah.

I couldn't help but scowl when I saw Sasha sitting on the couch, filing her nails. She was the only one in the room who seemed completely at ease, which felt so wrong after what Aiden had said outside.

Now that I thought about it, Sasha had been giving off bad vibes from the very beginning. I needed to know more about her and I needed to know soon. Aiden was enough of a mystery without throwing his sister into the mix.

Greg caught my gaze and smiled sadly before arranging his face into one filled with determination.

"So, are you planning on telling us what the hell happened last night?" he asked, bypassing any friendly chit-chat.

"Right to the point, I see," Aiden replied once he had everyone's attention. "I don't know what to say other than things got messy."

"Messy!" Greg stood up abruptly and balled his hands into fists. "My girlfriend was shot and we just left her there to die."

"We couldn't stay."

Greg shoved Aiden back until he was flat against the side of the wall. "Her mum called the cops and reported her missing this morning." Greg's voice shook. "She can't even look at me without crying."

"Please tell me you didn't tell the cops anything."

"That's what you care about?" Greg grabbed the front of Aiden's shirt as his face flushed with anger. "I'm so done with you. I'm done with all of you."

A tense silence filled the room. No one knew what to do or say to calm Greg down.

"I'm out of here," he spat, releasing Aiden and stomping toward the front door.

"Wait, we're not done yet."

"Like hell we aren't." Greg turned to Aiden with a snarl. "Give me one good reason why I shouldn't go to the cops."

"The Porsches we took belong to Bobby Zangari," he admitted. "I don't think I have to tell you how serious this is."

The anger drained from Greg's face, and without another word he sat back down on the couch and put his head in his hands.

"You're joking, right?" Noah finally asked, whipping his head around hoping that one of us might start laughing, his British accent growing thicker as panic set in. "What are we going to do?"

Aiden handed Noah the piece of paper that Dom had given us. Earlier, I had stuffed it in my pocket so quickly that I didn't notice that the only writing on the paper was a little 'X' in the corner of the page.

"What is this shit?" Libby called out, glaring at me as if it was my fault.

"It's our shopping list," Aiden replied without glancing her way.

Okay, what the hell was going on? The paper was practically blank. I mean, it didn't even have a logo on it or anything.

Noah approached the fireplace and held the paper up. As the heat radiated behind it, letters and numbers began to appear on the sheet in a pale beige colour. Soon enough, a list of twenty different makes and models of cars appeared. "Whoa." Greg peered over the corner of the couch and stared, completely mystified. "Magic?"

"Nope, just white wine." Aiden took hold of the list from Noah and stared intently at it. "Dom's always been a little paranoid."

Aiden went on to explain Dom's less-than-attractive offer.

"Why all at once?" Noah asked. "It'd be safer if we took a few cars over a couple of days instead of one big hit."

"Ideally, that would be great," Aiden said. "But we're dealing with the Mob here, Noah. Bobby won't hesitate to kill us if we mess him around."

There was an extremely uncomfortable silence as everybody took in the fact that if we failed to get this job done, we were screwed.

The only person who didn't seem fazed was Sasha. She was a lot like Aiden in her ability to hide how she really felt with a mask of indifference.

"Aiden always was good with a dramatic twist." Sasha finally piped up and joined the conversation. "Anyone have any suggestions?"

Oh, of course she'd try to take charge of this after bailing on us earlier. Why was no one else seeing her for what she really was?

I folded my arms in disapproval and frowned. I couldn't help blaming her for Brooke's death. She of all people knew how important the heist was and yet she abandoned us right in the middle of it. I was surprised that no one had brought it up. My only guess was that Aiden had talked to the others prior to the meeting.

Another thing that bothered me was the fact that she knew Bobby well enough to have something of his.

I refused to believe Aiden's crap about how it was all a misunderstanding. Why couldn't he see through her lies? Or was he lying to me to protect his sister?

"Couldn't we just take what we need from a parking lot somewhere?" Noah's voice broke through my daze and I realised that I had been staring at Sasha the entire time.

Awkward.

"There'd be so many cars that no one would really take notice of what we're doing until we're done."

"That would be perfect if we didn't have to collect specific types," Aiden replied, slipping Dom's list onto the coffee table in front of us. "She needs the parts for her clients so we have to work off this."

I leaned forward and peered at the list. Of the twenty cars on the list, I barely recognised one of them. According to the dates written beside the models, there were a few old ones dating back to the early nineties like the Toyota Supra, and newer models like the BMW Z4 and the Ford Mustang GT350R. None of the names really meant anything to me except for the Chevy Impala.

"Mr Cruz," I whispered.

"Huh?" Greg asked.

"Mr Cruz is my economics teacher," I explained. "He has a Chevy Impala. I'm not sure if it's the right model, but he has one."

"It's the right model," Noah chimed in. "I've seen it in the teacher's car park. Mrs Collins' car is also on this list. I helped the seniors move it last year as a prank."

"Could we find the others there as well?"

"Do you even know how rare these cars are?" Greg said, with bitterness in his voice. "There's no way we can get parts for any of these in Silverlake."

"We won't need these exact models, just cars that have parts that fit them." Noah slid his phone from his pocket and began typing vigorously. "They won't run as well or even fit perfectly but if we make the exchange quick, we can get out before Dom has a chance to really look at them."

"Dom's not an idiot, she'll know." Aiden frowned. "But she may not care what models we bring as long as the parts fit what she needs. She wants quality so the parts better fit right."

We may not have had a perfect plan but at least it was something. Noah continued to type on his phone, stopping every now and then to jot down a name. We knew the layout of the teacher's car park and we knew the teachers. The boys knew cars well enough to know what we'd expect to see in the car park.

Anyone could see that it was the best option for the time

frame we had. Well, maybe not everyone if the look Sasha was giving me was any indication.

"Nice work, genius," she sneered. "And how do you expect us to get away with stealing cars during the day, or does Silverlake hold all their classes at night now?"

Okay, so she had a point. What did she expect us to do? It was rare to find a large group of cars together late at night, let alone the ones that would have the parts we needed.

"Come on, Libs, you know it's our best option."

I was sure Libby would back me up on this. Even though things were tense right now, we were always there for each other. But instead of backing me up, she turned around and folded her arms.

That was it. After tonight, we were going to sort whatever it was that had her bitch meter stuck on "mega".

"Well, dear sister, what do you suggest then?" Aiden shot me a supportive look before turning back to Sasha.

"There's a dealership in the next town. All the models we need, all under one roof. It'll be perfect."

I stared at her. "How do you know they have what we need?"

"I did some work experience there a few years ago," she quipped, crossing her arms. "It's our best bet."

"No, it's not. Dealerships with expensive cars are bound to have expensive security systems."

"A camera and a gate is hardly Mission Impossible," she sneered. "Look, we'll go in, steal the rarest cars on the list and bargain with Dom. We can get in and out before anyone notices."

"Have you even met Dom? She's not going to bargain with us."

"I've been doing this a lot longer than you, sweetheart." Sasha eyed me up and down with distain. "People like Dom value money above all. We bring her rare cars and the promise of more, and she'll agree to it."

"Surely, I'm not the only one who thinks this idea is utter crap, right?"

I looked at each of them individually but it wasn't until my eyes landed on Libby that I realised I was outnumbered.

They were nervous but clearly, they had made their choice. We were going to collect these cars from a dealership, whether I thought it was a good idea or not.

* * *

Forty minutes later we were creeping towards Elcotron Motors. The dealership looked nothing like I had imagined it would. In my head, I saw a small business with cars covering every inch of its lawn and thick yellow prices drawn onto the windscreens. However, this dealership was exactly the opposite.

Elcotron Motors could have rivalled a hospital with how clean it was. Behind the metal chain rope pulled tightly across the entrance stood an empty car park and a tall glass building illuminated by the massive Elcotron Motors Corp sign. Unlike other car dealerships, Elcotron had their cars displayed inside the building. Some were parked neatly in rows next to waist high stands listing their features, while others were lifted on small ramps with suspension cords keeping them in place.

As if this wasn't going to be hard enough, Sasha had to choose a dealership that looked like a single speck of dust on their immaculate floor would get us caught.

"Let's go." Aiden's lips were so close to my ear that he made me flinch.

This was the first time that I hadn't helped make the plans and I wasn't so sure about the whole situation. It made me incredibly nervous.

Sasha had to be crazy. Anyone with eyes could see that stealing from Elcotron was going to be nearly impossible. They housed some of the most expensive cars that would ever drive through Silverlake.

Sure, stealing the cars from individual people would have been risky and time consuming, but at least we would have had a shot. I wasn't so sure whether we even had one with this plan.

Aiden tugged on my shirt to get my attention and it was then that I realised the others had moved. We were going to stay in a group for this heist, which was much riskier, but after what happened to Brooke, we weren't about to try splitting up again any time soon.

I followed Aiden towards the side of the building where the others had huddled. The lighting around the front of the dealership cast out shadows that covered the area, so we were hidden from any passers-by. Aiden stopped to peer through the front window and scan the silent room of cars briefly before he tugged me forward.

The side wall wasn't made out of glass like the front of the building. Instead, it was the typical dull grey concrete most buildings were constructed from. Our group headed towards a small door; to its right was a keypad in a similar shade of grey to the rest of the building. A red light flickered above the numbered buttons.

"Just a camera and a gate huh?" I spat at Sasha, staring at the keypad with distain.

"They must have updated their security system after I left." Sasha wore a surprised expression but it just looked fake to me. "Whoops, sorry guys."

"So what do we do now?" Greg's voice raised in panic.

I had nothing. There was a massive passcode-protected door in our way and I was all out of ideas.

Noah kneeled down in front of the door and pulled his backpack off his shoulder. He rummaged around until he gave up with a sigh and turned towards us.

"Have any of you ladies got any talcum powder or dry shampoo in those bags of yours? I thought I had some deodorant in mine but I'm out."

"No, why?" I asked.

"I need something with a powder base, anything will do."

Libby pulled her bag off and began to search through the side flap. "I've got my foundation, will that work?" she said, pulling out the small blue compact she used for touch ups.

With a slight nod, Noah took the compact and scraped a chunk of it into his hands, then crushed it into a loose powder.

"Seriously?" Libby's voice was thick with a mix of sarcasm and barely veiled anger. "This isn't the time for a make-up lesson."

Noah glanced at her with a sour expression that made her shrink back slightly.

That was weird. I don't think I've ever met someone who had the ability to make Libby feel embarrassed about her insults. Whatever was going on with them earlier was obviously still unresolved. I raised my hand to place on her shoulder in comfort, but she tensed.

"I'm using the powder to dust the keypad, so no, we're not doing our make-up, Libby," Noah snapped. In the short time that I had known him, he had never once lost his temper. "Our fingers leave residue behind whenever we touch something. We'll be able to tell which numbers make up the passcode."

Once again, I was left trying to figure Noah out. He was incredibly smart and seemed to know a lot about breaking into things. Aiden had told me that they'd met at a New Year's Eve party last year. I still wasn't so sure about his motive for being part of the heist, but Aiden had said that Noah wanted to feel something for once and that I should leave it alone.

Like I could just forget. I'd find out what his story was eventually, but right now, it was time to get through this stupid heist and be done with it.

As Noah brushed the make-up lightly across the keys, I could see which numbers the powder clung to in clumps.

"Dude, that's totally some *Mission Impossible* magic you're doing right there," Greg said in a loud whisper.

Noah smiled at him and turned back to the keypad. He continued to dust the keys until four were covered in a thin layer of powder; fingerprints clear on the buttons.

Okay, so we now knew the numbers, but what good were they going to be to us if we didn't know the sequence in which they had to be entered? It was common sense that the passcode would lock after only a few failed attempts, so we had to get this right.

I can't have been the only one looking confused because Noah shook his head before explaining that most corporate codes were designed from left to right and top to bottom.

"It's as common as using your birth date as your computer password," Noah said. He swiftly tapped the sequence in and a sharp metal click rang out, unlocking the door.

Well, that was far too quick for my liking. This entire heist just didn't feel right and if the doubt swirling inside my stomach was anything to go by, the whole thing should be anything but easy.

"Right, here's the plan," Aiden spoke up. "Noah's going to hack the system and get the main doors open without setting the alarm off. We'll be taking the cars in a similar fashion to the first heist, but we'll be working alone."

This was crazy. We lost Brooke and barely even made it through the first heist; he was insane if he thought we could pull this off individually. We didn't even have the benefit of an open environment. We were like trapped animals hoping not to be mauled to death.

"Noah will tap into the police scanner to keep track of any alerts," Aiden continued. "Greg, from what I saw through the window, your car is attached to a suspension board. Make sure you remove the cable before you go anywhere."

Without another word, everyone made their way through the door. We followed a long corridor until we reached the showroom.

There were so many cars. I couldn't even tell which ones were our targets and which ones were extras. They all looked the same to me. With a tap to my shoulder, Aiden pointed towards a dark red compact car sitting in the corner. Once I was closer, I noticed the Mitsubishi symbol and the Mirage label above it. I was grateful that it was small enough for me to manoeuvre through this place.

The others had reached their own cars and were working on getting them open. Aiden broke into his black sedan without much effort. Greg was the next to get his car going, and Libby was about to crack hers when static filled the room.

If I thought I knew what real fear felt like before, I was wrong. Real fear was hearing the security guard informing the police that there were intruders in the building. Real fear was seeing the light from a torch bounce off the windows from the corridor we had entered.

"Shit!" Noah shoved his scanner back into his bag and swung it around his shoulders. "We have to get out of here, now!"

The sound of jingling keys was lost in our scurry to get moving. Libby and I were both still struggling to jimmy the locks on our cars, but it was pointless to keep trying now. Aiden hailed us over to get into his car and as I was passing, I saw Greg attempting to start Sasha's car.

"We don't have time for this," Sasha called out. "Move." She pushed past Greg and slid into the driver's side of his car. She didn't even wait for him. Without glancing our way, she slammed the door shut and stomped her foot on the accelerator, making the tyres screech and the car lurch forward.

I didn't see the cord until the moment it snapped. The same cord that Greg was supposed to have removed. It severed from the car's rear and rebounded off the boot, smacking Greg against his temple. Either the world had stopped or someone had hit the pause button on our disastrous movie. Everything seemed to stop. All of us stood frozen beside Greg as a gush of crimson spread down his face and he fell to the ground.

There was so much blood. God, how was it even possible for a body to hold that much blood? I kneeled down next to Greg and pressed my hand tightly against the gash on his head. His blood seeped through my fingers and I fought the urge to vomit.

The place was in utter chaos. Libby was screaming, her entire body shaking from the force of her lungs. Aiden and Noah stood quietly by my side, no colour in their faces except for the pale clammy white that was left after the shock set in.

The sound of the security alarm ringing through the building was the only thing that brought me back to what was happening. Why was no one moving? I fought to control the bleeding but it was clear that we needed to get help. We couldn't call an ambulance for obvious reasons so it was time to get creative.

"Noah, shut Libby up and bring Aiden's car around now."

"Oi, you lot, stop right there." The burly security guard ran towards us from the back of the room, shoving his walkie talkie into his holster.

Aiden helped me lift Greg into the backseat of the car and we were soon flying out of the dealership to the sound of the alarm blaring.

"Where are we going?" Noah asked shakily, his hands gripping the steering wheel.

"The hospital."

The others looked at me with a mix of fear and confusion. Of course we couldn't go to the hospital without having to explain exactly what had happened and I didn't plan on doing that. But we did need to get Greg help or he was going to die.

We raced through the streets under the sickly orange streetlights. No one said a word. I hoped Noah knew where he was going, but I was too busy concentrating on Greg to ask. I couldn't feel much of a heartbeat anymore. I brushed my fingers against his neck, but the hectic thumping that was there earlier was now too light to feel.

Please don't die, please hold on. I didn't think I could cope with another death after Brooke's. How many minutes could someone survive with the blood that was supposed to be flowing through his veins now dribbling warmly down my jeans?

Eventually Noah took a sharp right and I saw the familiar blue and white 'H' sign. As we pulled up to the hospital's emergency entrance, I made a decision. Without another word, I removed my hands from Greg's wound and pushed the door open.

"What are you doing?" Aiden called out.

There was no way I could answer him without making myself sick, so I ignored his question and gripped tightly onto Greg's shoulders. Pulling with all my strength, I dragged him from the seat and dropped him on the ground. The light thump of his body hitting the footpath finally made the darkness that had filled me fall away.

Oh god. What the hell was I doing? I knew this was the best decision, but it didn't make me feel any less like a monster. Without another word, I shuffled back into the car and reached into the front to beep the horn.

"Go, Noah, now." I wasn't completely heartless. Someone would have heard the car horn and would come out and find Greg. I wouldn't leave him to die.

Someone would come.

They'd have to, right?

Greg's blood was drying in between my shaking fingers. I couldn't stop rubbing my hands. I felt so dirty. The crack of the cable smacking into Greg's face kept vibrating through my mind and I couldn't seem to take in a full breath. I was suffocating from my own thoughts.

A warm hand took hold of mine and I tore my gaze from the window to look at Aiden. Why was he trying to comfort me when I was such a terrible person? I should have taken Greg into the emergency room instead of leaving him. However, I chose to put the heist before his life—my own life before his.

What kind of person did that make me? Something had snapped inside of me and I was suddenly becoming this ruthless cold-hearted beast. I wasn't going to let Greg's injury get in the way of achieving our heist.

Sure, I was incredibly ambitious, but I also believed in compassion and love. I tried to comfort myself by remembering that there were more lives involved than just mine and Greg's. I had Libby, Aiden and Noah to think about, too. But it wasn't them I was thinking about as I pushed Greg on to the footpath—just myself.

"We're here." Noah's broken voice filled the silence that had formed between us.

I tore myself out of my thoughts to see that Noah had driven us back to Sasha's house. The house was dark, and neither the car nor Sasha were anywhere to be seen. I wonder if she even knew what had happened. If she had, why didn't she stop? God, I just wanted my head to stop spinning with questions and accusations. I just wanted to go home.

"So, what now?" Libby asked. The screaming had left her voice a little hoarse, but she took on an angry tone that made no sense to me.

"We go for plan B." Aiden had returned to his usual demeanour. It was like he never allowed himself to feel anything. Or maybe he just couldn't feel anything. "We still need to finish this job and we have another eight cars to collect."

"Yeah, because the first plan went so damn well," Libby quipped. "So enlighten us Aiden, what's your next brilliant plan?"

Anger grew deeper in her voice and once again I was left trying to work out where it was all coming from. She had chosen to be part of this so it wasn't like she could play innocent.

"We're going to go with the plan we should have followed from the beginning." Aiden kept his eyes on me while he spoke to Noah. "Do you think it's possible to find the parts we need in the teachers' car park?"

"It'll be tricky, but if we go back a few years in the models we'll find something," he replied.

"How are we supposed to steal all nine cars without getting caught?" I rubbed my forehead, the start of a migraine well on its way. "Brooke is gone, Greg is injured and Sasha is who knows where. There aren't enough of us."

"We already have this so we only need eight more." Aiden clasped his hands together and lowered his hand into them. "Sasha will show up, I trust her. She won't let us down. We'll just have to make two trips."

"You're kidding, right?"

"We'll just have to make it work. We're running out of options here."

"I'll make a list of the teachers that have the cars we need." Noah's body relaxed at the opportunity for a distraction. "They have to register their cars with the school so all I have to do is access their files and search for the cars we need."

"You're serious about this? You're talking about stealing from our teachers," Libby exclaimed. "Don't you think that's going too far? It's bad enough to take from strangers, but these are people we know."

She did have a point. They were people we saw every day

and I could already feel the guilt forming. But there was no other choice. We'd botched our first attempt and Greg was now lying in the hospital bleeding. At least we knew the place and the dangers. No one else was going to die. I couldn't handle any more death.

"I'm with Aiden on this one."

Whoa, the speed at which Libby's face turned cold was ridiculous. Her lips pulled together as if she has just sucked on a lemon and her eyes blazed with anger and hurt.

I felt like someone had punched me in the stomach. What was happening with us? We used to be in sync. Surely she knew we were out of options.

"Fine," she said abruptly. "I'm going inside." Without glancing our way, she stormed from the front seat and disappeared into the house. I wanted to go and sort everything out with her, but I knew it was pointless. Once Libby was upset over something there was no point trying to fix it until she had time to calm down.

Taking a moment to control the ache in my chest, I waited for someone to talk.

"Right, I think Nic and I should scope out the car park tomorrow morning before anyone gets there," Aiden stated after the silence had lingered too long. "I have a free period first thing so I'll stay behind and keep watch while the rest of you go to class. That way I can make sure any obstacles are dealt with before we make our move."

"I'll meet up with you after the bell rings," Noah added, cracking his knuckles. "Got to make sure someone is watching your back while you're watching ours."

I tuned out after agreeing with Aiden. I didn't know what I was supposed to do anymore. Every time we thought we were finished, something would remind us just how little control we really had. I didn't know how much longer I could do this and keep myself from turning into someone that I never wanted to be.

* * *

By the time the clock chimed at midnight, we had migrated inside to figure out exactly how we were going to collect the remaining cars.

"So you and Libby will go to your classes like it's a normal day. Wait for my text, then ask to be excused," Aiden said. "It'll be better if you aren't absent. They won't suspect you."

"What about you guys?" I asked, looking at Aiden and Noah. Sasha still hadn't returned, and with Aiden frequently eyeing the door, it was clear he didn't know where she was either.

"I ditch class so often that it would be odd if I was there. And Noah's home with the flu," Aiden smirked. "Or at least that'll be what the school will think when I leave a voicemail on the school's hotline."

I nodded, too focused on the plan to frown at Aiden's lack of attendance. "How's this going to work?"

With a dull smile, Aiden leaned back in his chair, stretching his tired muscles after sitting still for so long. "We're going to take four cars first and then come back for the last four," he said. "Someone will need to stay behind to keep watch in between pickups, but we'll work out who on the day."

I nodded in agreement and listened to the rest of the plan. Everything seemed to be perfect except for the fact that we would have to do the entire heist in broad daylight, with a school full of students and teachers nearby. It wasn't the most ideal setting, but it was the only choice we had.

"Well, I think that's about it," Aiden said, folding the car list up and shifting out of his chair. "I better get you two home before your parents wake up and find you missing."

Libby lifted herself from the couch where she had been blatantly ignoring us and walked out the front door.

I rose from my chair and smiled sadly at Aiden. With Libby's constant anger and Sasha's disappearing act, I'm sure he was sick of us girls by now. With that thought in mind, I came up with an idea that might just crack the mystery that was Sasha.

"Hey guys, I'm just going to use the bathroom," I said, waving the others off. "I'll meet you outside, Aiden."

He nodded and exited the house, leaving me on my own. Instead of going left for the bathroom, I headed to the right for the room that could only be Sasha's.

Everyone knew that a person's bedroom reflected the basis of their personality and, of course, their secrets. Okay, so I knew snooping was socially taboo, but I had to know who I was dealing with. There was something about Sasha that wasn't sitting right with me.

The first thing I noticed when I walked in was the massive steel frame bed taking up half the room. The wall paint was sheer black and made the room feel cold and uninviting. I didn't know what I was looking for or whether my suspicion was even real, but I couldn't stop myself from exploring further. I scanned the room and my eyes landed on a bedside table with a couple of empty wooden photo frames sitting on top of it.

That just upped the creepy factor. I walked to the table and carefully opened the top drawer. At first, it appeared empty except for a few out of date fashion magazines and an old bottle of dark blue nail polish.

Nothing strange there. I started to close the drawer and accept that I was overreacting when a strange feeling struck me. Something didn't feel right about the magazines. I didn't know Sasha well, but she didn't seem like the *Vogue* type.

Before I could chicken out, I reopened the drawer and

grabbed the magazines. A large metal object fell to the floor with a loud thud and I bent to pick it up.

No way.

It couldn't be.

Holy cow, it was.

I felt my blood rush to my ears and my stomach fall through the floor.

I was holding a gun.

Was this a damn episode of *Breaking Bad*? Why was everyone suddenly packing heat around here? I quickly dropped the gun back into the drawer and covered it up with the magazines. Stumbling back a few steps, I landed on the bed. I tried to relax my body with a few deep breaths but it was pointless. I didn't know why Sasha needed a gun, but I could only guess that it wasn't for anything good. Because really, what good could be achieved with a gun?

"Nic, we really need to leave." Aiden's voice filtered through the house from the front door, making me jump.

I couldn't tell anyone about this, at least not until I knew what it was for. After all, how could I really know whether Aiden already knew and just wasn't telling me for some reason, or if he really was clueless about it all?

I shuddered as I walked back out to the others, rearranging my face into a relaxed expression as best I could. My mind was racing as my heart pounded. Sasha had a gun; if that told me one thing, it was that she couldn't be trusted, now more than ever.

* * *

With only a few hours left until we were going to attempt the most difficult heist I had ever thought imaginable, I found it nearly impossible to fall asleep. Our targets were going to be the teachers we saw every day. How was I going to be able to look them in the face and act like nothing happened after this?

Aiden had dropped us off just a little after midnight and Libby walked quietly into the spare room without even looking my way. She had been mad all day.

I just didn't understand. Whenever we had disagreed in the past, we always managed to avoid fighting. This time it felt like I was missing something. I fidgeted in my bed until I finally lay flat on my back under a thin blanket. The only light in the room came from the flashing standby light of my laptop and the moon outside my window.

Although the room was silent, it seemed like my brain just wouldn't shut up. I knew the school heist was going to be tricky and we would need to be extremely lucky to succeed. What I didn't know was whether I should be concerned about Sasha. Aiden was so sure that she would be there to help us, but I wasn't convinced. She had a gun—how was that ever a good sign? The only people with guns around here were the police or people who didn't have good intentions.

Libby would tell me that I was overthinking things as usual and proceed to make wild assumptions about why Sasha needed a gun. My chest tightened at the thought of Libby and how she wouldn't even look at me anymore. Lying here and trying to fall asleep was never going to happen until I had worked things out with her. If I didn't want to look like a cast member of *The Walking Dead* from lack of sleep, I had to talk to her now.

Lifting myself out of bed, I stumbled to my door and tiptoed across the hall to Libby's room. Pushing the door open slowly, I saw her sitting on the bed and reading the latest *Harry Potter* book.

"Hey," I said hesitantly from the doorway. "You got a minute?"

"Better make it quick," she said, placing her book down on the bed to face me with a stone still expression. "What is it?"

Although she didn't exactly say anything mean, her tone was flat and her face uninviting.

I walked into the room and perched myself onto the end of the bed. "Are you okay?" I asked after a short silence. "We haven't really talked since Aiden picked us up and I feel like you are avoiding me a little."

"I don't know what you're talking about," she said a little too defensively. "I've been by your side all night."

"You may have been by my side but you won't talk or even look at me."

She crossed her arms against herself and the ice in her eyes gave me an eerie chill. "I'm talking to you right now."

"You know what I mean," I said. "Is this about Aiden?"

A scowl spread across her face and I knew that he had something to do with it. "No, it's not about your stupid boyfriend," she spat. "Nothing is wrong, so just drop it." She stood abruptly and walked to the small desk in the corner of the room.

"No, I'm not going to drop it," I said stubbornly. "It's obvious that you have an issue with me."

She spun around to face me with murderous eyes. I had only ever seen Libby this mad once, back in our first year of high school when Justin Summers tried to splash water on her white dress shirt as a prank.

"Oh yeah, because there's no way a parent's wet dream like you could do anything wrong!" she replied venomously. "You've got it all figured out."

"God, what is wrong with you?" I asked. "Why are you being such a colossal bitch?"

"Bloody hell!" She threw her hands in the air and turned away from me. "Nothing is wrong."

"If nothing is wrong then you wouldn't be avoiding me," I exclaimed. "What happened to us against the world?" By now, my heart was beating so fast that the only thing I could hear was the rush of blood behind my ears. I took a few shallow breaths and my vision blurred with unshed tears.

Libby snapped her head up to look at me and I saw hurt threaded through her fury. "Oh, so now we're the dynamic duo again?" she argued, placing her hands on her hips. "Now you want to be a team?"

Okay, she had really lost me this time. I always wanted us to be a team. Nothing had changed that. "What are you talking about?"

Libby narrowed her eyes and pursed her lips so tightly that they started to go white around the edges. "Ever since Aiden took us on, you haven't had my back," she explained. "We haven't been the dynamic duo in a long time and I don't think you even care."

"That's not true."

"Isn't it? You made the decision to go after the teacher's cars without even talking to me about it.

"We didn't have a choice in that."

"And who's to blame for that?" she retorted. "You claim that we're still a team but I don't recall being there when you visited Dom and made a deal that the whole group really should have been a part of. Face it, we haven't been a team since the moment this all started."

Libby's anger seemed to melt more into disappointment and I felt shame seep into my body. I didn't realise that I was making her feel like she wasn't important to me. It wasn't fair that she thought I had a choice in all of this though.

"You know we had to do it."

"God, I wish I had never gotten us involved in the first place."

Wait a minute. What did she mean by that? We didn't have a choice, Aiden made sure of that. I was there the night we were forced into this. She didn't get involved in the conversation until we had made the deal with Aiden.

Before I had a chance to say anything, her mouth snapped shut and she stared at me with wide eyes. It was the same look she had whenever I retold her embarrassing pre-period stories.

"What?"

"Nothing! Just leave me alone, would you?"

I sighed. Libby was clearly still hiding something.

"Fine," I said. "See you in the morning."

I went back to my bed and tried to get comfortable, as if that was possible after the day I'd had. I tossed and turned for what felt like hours. I only realised I'd been sleeping at all when a piercing scream woke me up.

I rushed out into the hall. The scream had come from the spare room. I could hear my parents moving around.

"It's all right!" I called. "Libby's just having a nightmare. We watched a horror film earlier." Man, I hoped it was just a nightmare. I nipped into Libby's room before Mum and Dad could come out and start asking questions.

Libby was sitting up in bed, crying. I sat down on the bed and put my arm around her shoulders.

"What is it? What happened?"

"It was Greg," she sobbed. I could see her trying to pull herself together, but she was obviously still frightened. "He was bleeding out, and I was driving him to the hospital, but then he was you, and I couldn't find the hospital, and you were dying …" She took a deep breath and looked me straight in the eye. "Nic, that thing I said earlier about getting us into this … I was the one who told Aiden about Murdoch."

Wait, what? How could Libby go so low as to use that against me? She knew how much it meant to me. I could understand wanting to be popular, but this was psychotic.

"Oh, don't look so damn shocked," Libby said defensively, rubbing away her tears.

"Why would you do that?" I stammered.

"Because I am sick of being a nobody in this stupid hick town," she exploded. The tear stains on her face undermined her snarkiness and gave her an almost vulnerable look. "You have these big dreams of getting out of here and I'm going to be left behind."

Oh.

I should have been angry at her for everything we'd been through, but I knew Libby hadn't meant for any of this to happen. Except maybe I didn't know as much as I thought I had. Otherwise, I would have seen how lonely she was. I always thought she understood my desire to get out of Silverlake. I didn't realise that she might have wanted to get out as well.

"Libs ..." I started, trying to think of a way to make her see that we were always going to be the dynamic duo. However, her moment of vulnerability was quickly closed off and she tensed, the hurt in her eyes fading back into anger.

"Save it," she spat. "I'm not interested. Just leave me alone." She gave me one last look and turned her back to me, pulling the covers up until I couldn't see her face. Reaching up, she switched the lamp off and plunged the room into darkness.

Shit. I was completely lost now. It wasn't like there was a manual on how to repair this kind of damage. Exhaling a broken breath, I left the room in silence. The ache I felt in my stomach before was back, and as I fell into bed I knew it wasn't going to fade anytime soon.

13
The Big Day

Bzzzt! My alarm went off at 6 am, jolting me from a nightmare plagued with police officers and Bobby's henchmen. I sat up in my bed and pulled my hair from the base of my sweat soaked neck. It was only a nightmare but my arms still shook with adrenaline.

My phone vibrated loudly on my bedside table, making me jump. Taking a deep breath, I reached over to see a message from Aiden.

> **Hey Bonnie, today's the day. I'm picking you up at 7am. No arguments—Clyde**

A small chuckle slipped out of my sleep hoarse throat.

Hang on … was Aiden suggesting that we were a couple? There was no doubt things between us had become confusing, but every time we got close Aiden was quick to shut it down.

"Nicole, get your butt out of bed or you'll be late," Mum called from outside my bedroom door. "Wake Libby up as well, will you?"

My stomach did an obnoxious somersault and all I could manage was a quick muffled reply. I had forgotten about the massive blow out we had last night. Since the first time I met Libby, we had never once had a fight or even a disagreement that went beyond bickering over our favourite television shows and crushes. This was completely new territory for me and I had no idea how I was supposed to deal with it.

Maybe I was supposed to apologise and let it go, or maybe

I was supposed to ice her out and teach her a lesson. Why couldn't someone have taught a class on how best to go about fighting with the closest people in your life? It would have been a huge help right about then.

Rubbing my face roughly, I climbed out of bed and lifted my school uniform from where it was draped over my computer chair. The walk to the bathroom was hazy, considering I couldn't get out of my thoughts long enough to register what was happening.

I tried to open the door three times before I realised that it was locked. With the pop music blaring from behind the door, it could only mean one thing.

Libby was inside.

The bathroom had a shower area separate from the vanity so Libby and I were able to use it at the same time and still have our privacy. Our bathroom ritual included never locking the door on each other.

So it was official; she was still pissed with me.

"Really, Libby?" I yelled over her hair dryer. "You're seriously still mad?"

When she didn't reply, I huffed loudly and stomped downstairs to use the main bathroom. What the hell gave her the right to act like this in my house? She was the one who lied, not me. Why didn't she understand that?

I showered quickly and threw my school uniform on, running my hands through my hair and pulling it up into a loose bun. Taking a few minutes to apply my make-up, I shuffled my way into the kitchen. Mum had already made banana pancakes and the aroma was intoxicating.

It was a trap of course. Mum only made pancakes when she wanted to talk about something. Seeing no point in delaying what was bound to come, I placed my backpack near my chair and sat down at the table.

"Is everything okay with you and Lib?" Mum peered at me over her coffee cup.

I took my time reaching for a pancake and drowning it in syrup. I'd do just about anything to delay this conversation. "We're fine."

"If you're so fine," Mum said, "why are you showering down here?"

I shrugged my shoulders, silently begging her to drop the subject. Couldn't she see I didn't want to talk? Even if I could tell her why Lib and weren't talking to each other, it wouldn't help.

"Well whatever it is, I'm sure it's not worth throwing away your friendship. Just remember that."

I stared at my plate blankly, taking in what she said. What Libby did was hurtful and practically deluded. We could have died. I mean, Brooke *actually* died, and who knew how Greg was doing? I couldn't even look in the mirror anymore without being sick with the person I had become.

But Libby had made one valid point. I had been acting like I'd forgotten about our dynamic duo. I'd made her feel as if we were drifting apart and that she was alone. For a girl who had issues with being left behind, feeling lonely would have been a good enough reason to do just about anything.

I quickly looked up when Libby walked through the door, dressed and ready to go. She avoided my eyes as she sat down across from me and piled two pancakes onto a plate.

"So, busy day today, girls?" Mum asked after clearing her throat. Even she could feel the tension between us.

"Not really," Libby replied nonchalantly. "Just the usual classes, so it should be pretty quiet."

Great, she was still refusing to make eye contact, even when I pushed the syrup her way. She clenched her jaw in between bites and tensed her shoulders so tightly she'd probably end up with sore muscles later. This had gone on long enough. We needed to talk before things got any more strained.

"Well, I think I'd better make my way to work. You girls behave yourselves."

It's like Mum knew what I was thinking.

With Mum gone, the kitchen was silent and the air seemed almost too thick to breathe. I waited for Libby to be the first to break, but when a few seconds went by and she continued to keep her eyes trained on her pancakes I couldn't wait any longer.

"Libs …" I started timidly, releasing a breath I didn't know I was holding.

"Nope." She dropped her knife and fork with a loud clatter and pushed her chair out suddenly. "I'm not interested in anything you have to say."

"We need to talk about this."

I caught a hint of sadness in her face but it was quickly replaced with indifference only a second later.

"There's nothing to talk about, Nic," she said coolly, hauling her bag over her shoulder. "Look, I know how important today is and I'll do my part of the plan but once this mess is over and we get our lives back, I want you to leave me alone."

What was this, a soap opera? My stomach churned so fast that I felt slightly dizzy and my heart pounded painfully. I hated feeling like this, but wrestling a crocodile would have been easier than trying to get Libby to talk when she wasn't ready. The only option left was to let it go and come back to it once she'd had a chance to process everything. Besides, we had much bigger things to deal with.

Her phone started beeping loudly from her pocket. She pulled it out and turned to leave.

"Where are you going?" I asked breathlessly.

"I'm catching a lift with Noah," she said with a flat tone. "I'll see you and Aiden at the side gate when he gives the signal."

"Since when did you two sort things out?"

"Not that it's any of your business but I called him last night and we talked. I apologised and he forgave me."

"What, so you can work things out with him but you won't with me?"

Without replying, she walked out of the kitchen and exited the house. I sat there for a few minutes trying to relax my body. Things had gone from bad to catastrophic in less than twenty-four hours. We still had Bobby breathing down our necks and if we didn't pull this job off we'd also have Dom and her ladies to deal with. My breathing hitched and I felt the familiar sting at the back of my eyes. Before any tears could form, I blinked them back down. I hadn't allowed myself to cry since Brooke was shot and I wasn't going to start now.

Picking up my bag and locking the front door, I paced slowly outside while I waited for Aiden. There was a weight in my stomach that was making me sick. I knew it was nerves, but there seemed to be something else as well. Call it women's intuition or whatever, but no matter what happened today, things were going to be different.

"Hey, Bonnie, thinking a bit hard there aren't we?" I jumped when I heard Aiden's smooth voice. I didn't even hear him pull up. "Get in, beautiful, we've got some teachers to mess with."

Really? He was making a joke at a time like this?

I frowned at him as he laughed and slid into the passenger's seat, securing my seatbelt. "Very funny."

Staring at the glove compartment, I felt Aiden's warm hands on my face, his calloused fingers tilting my chin until I was looking at him.

"What's wrong?"

What was with everyone asking me that? Was I seriously that transparent? I removed his hands from my face and motioned for him to start driving.

"It's a long story," I said as he reversed out of my driveway.

"We've got time, Nic."

There was no point hiding anything from Aiden. He could read my every emotion just by looking at me.

* * *

"I can't believe you find this funny." I raised my voice, trying to talk over Aiden's laughter. "It's not funny!" I scowled and waited for him to get himself under control.

He cleared his throat but still had a playful smile on his face. "I'm sorry," he said sincerely. "I just can't believe how dramatic you ladies are."

"What are you talking about? She's the one who lied to me."

"Yeah, but who hasn't lied before?"

Of course he'd say that. He built this entire operation on lies. In fact, I didn't even know if there was a time when he was being completely honest.

I exhaled loudly and rubbed my forehead in frustration. "I suppose."

I pushed back in my seat and took in my surroundings. The car idled in the staff car park's drop off bay. Aiden had planned to drop me off and park the car around the corner, but we had been sidetracked by my disagreement with Libby. Being seen together was risky, especially somewhere we weren't supposed to be.

I glanced towards the cars belonging to those teachers who insisted on arriving an hour before their students even woke up. Two of our chosen cars were already parked neatly in their assigned spaces. Mr Cruz's black Chevy Impala was shining delicately in the sun and small waves of heat shimmered off its hood.

Mr Johnson's Nissan Navara sat at a slight angle. Just like his car, Mr Johnson seemed out of place amongst the older, more experienced teachers. He seemed caught between being a teacher and still being young enough to be the student.

I rubbed my hand subconsciously along the armrest of Aiden's Lancer. Everything about his car screamed Aiden. It was beautiful but dark—a mystery to almost everyone.

"What are you thinking about?" Aiden said, pulling me from my thoughts.

"I'm thinking about you, me, the gang, today's plan, and the future," I rattled on. I smiled lazily as I held his gaze.

"So, not a whole lot then?" he joked, his smile not quite reaching his eyes.

"What's wrong?"

He wasn't the only one who could read people. His angular eyebrows knitted together in frustration and his eyes were drowning in pain. He sighed and turned his body to face me.

"I messed up."

Well, I wasn't expecting that, nor was I really sure what he was getting at. The plan was as close to perfect as we were ever going to get and the team was ready. After Brooke's death and Greg's injuries, we needed a way out of this mess and this had to be it.

When I didn't reply, Aiden ran a hand through his dark curls and took a deep breath in. "I promised that I wouldn't let anyone hurt you."

"And you haven't."

"Can't you see that I'm letting you get hurt?"

"I don't understand," I said, more confused than ever. "What's this all about?"

Aiden exhaled roughly and pulled his lips together until they moulded into a thin line. There was sadness in his eyes and along with something else—something dark.

A part of me wanted to reach out and touch him or comfort him—anything to get rid of that hint of guilt in his eyes.

Another part of me felt queasy, as if I had just gone for a ride on a roller coaster with one too many loops. I laid my hand softly on his bicep, and he tensed briefly before relaxing into my touch.

"I promised that you wouldn't get hurt, but that's exactly what I've been doing," Aiden explained, dropping his gaze to stare at my hand on his arm. "I lied to get you to agree to come to Sasha's and then I didn't give you a chance to walk away. I'm the reason we have to do this today … yet I don't even feel that bad about it, nor would I change it."

Sometimes I thought there were two versions of Aiden. There was the sweet and at the same time infuriating side that everyone got to see, and then there was this much more sinister side that seemed to come out whenever we were dealing with Bobby or Dom. This side seemed to shut off all empathy and act purely on impulse. It was rare to see this version of Aiden, but it was definitely there.

"I hate that I forced you into this, but I'm not sorry that we're here now."

"You're not sorry that we're about to steal from our teachers?" I asked timidly, not entirely sure I wanted to know the answer.

"Nope," he said nonchalantly.

Silence fell between us and I took a moment to take in what he was saying. When I had called Aiden dark, I meant it. He had light in him as well, but it seemed like his darkness overtook it at times. I should've been scared of him, or at least angry for what he had dragged me into, but I wasn't. He had shown me a whole new life full of possibilities, and I certainly couldn't hate him for that.

"Everyone has a dark side, Aiden." I gripped his arm lightly in reassurance. "Loving someone means loving everything about them, including the darker parts."

"Can you love mine?"

I looked up to meet Aiden's eyes and for the first time I saw a sliver of vulnerability. I knew the type of person Aiden was.

And I wasn't silly. I knew that he was not going to suddenly become a saint like all the bad boys in the movies did. He wasn't going to apologise for stealing the mob's cars and he certainly wasn't going to apologise for what we were going to do to our teachers.

I knew that and so did Aiden. He was asking me whether I could take him as he was.

I smiled briefly and tucked a piece of hair behind my ear. I knew my answer almost the second Aiden had asked the question. Before I could overthink it, I leaned forward and touched my lips to his. I didn't expect fireworks or anything like that—this wasn't a romance novel—but my lips did tingle pleasantly from the brief connection.

Just as soon as it happened, I withdrew and sat back in my seat, heat rising up my neck.

"Did you just kiss me?" Aiden asked incredulously.

"Yes I did, Mr Oblivious."

He frowned slightly with a mixture of confusion and surprise. "But that was your first kiss ..." he babbled. It was actually quite hilarious seeing him so flustered when usually he was so under control.

"Yes it was."

"But why?" he asked. "I don't understand."

"Because you saw something in me that no one else did," I said. "You took a quiet, disinterested girl and challenged her. You keep reminding me of the strength and courage I have and most importantly, you made me feel safe and warm inside even when everything was falling apart."

I drew a shaky breath in and felt relief pour though me. It felt good to finally get everything out. Aiden sat there with a stunned expression on his face. Then he locked his eyes with mine and broke into a huge grin.

"So does this mean you'll be my Bonnie after all?" he asked with a mischievous smirk.

Oh my god. I had feelings for a complete goofball. He caught my hand as I playfully went to slap his shoulder and he laced his fingers through mine.

"Of course, dork," I quipped.

"That's Clyde to you, ma'am," he said in the best cowboy accent he could muster. "Now that we're partners in crime and romance, I think we need to redo your first kiss."

"Excuse me?"

Aiden's eyes zeroed in on mine and the hazel darkened to a whiskey colour. They were so intense I didn't dare look away.

"A first kiss should be memorable," he said softly. "Let me make it worth remembering."

Aiden leaned over until I could feel the brief touch of his lips and his breath ghosting over mine. It felt like the first time I was in his car except this time there were no distractions or playful words. This time, it was pure anticipated passion.

"Relax," Aiden whispered gently against my lips. He slid his hand over my cheek with his fingers spread out, caressing my soft skin with his calloused hands. "I'm not going to hurt you, remember?"

"I know." I breathed brokenly. I didn't have a single clue what I was doing. This wasn't some romantic comedy where violins were going to play in the background. This was real. "I just …"

"Shh," Aiden cut in soothingly. "Just trust me."

Before I could reply, his lips were pressing lightly on mine. His hand slid from my cheek to rest against my neck. I could feel my heartbeat pulsating under his touch. He increased the pressure against my lips, which melted me into his grip. On instinct, I lifted my hands and placed one on his bicep and the other in his hair. I don't know why but I wanted to know how it felt to run my hands through his thick curls.

Oh wow, that was the tip of his tongue darting across my lips. I thought kissing would be disgusting because really, how sexy could tongue, saliva and dry lips be? I was wrong, obviously, because Aiden's lips were soft and pulsing slightly against mine. When his teeth nipped lightly at my bottom lip, my mouth parted slightly in surprise and Aiden took the opportunity to slide his tongue in a little.

Aiden may be cold when it came to everything else, but right in that moment he was gentle and even a little hesitant.

Of all the first kisses in the world, mine had to be at least in the top five. The air was thick with warmth and I could feel my entire body tingle. It was slightly awkward in the beginning with the hand brake between us. However, now it was completely forgotten.

An impatient knock against my window brought us back and we jumped apart. Seriously? They couldn't give us just a few more minutes?

I peered behind me and saw Sasha with her arms crossed tightly against her chest and a sour look on her face. Of course she would be the one to find us.

"You're supposed to be parking the car, not sucking faces," she argued once Aiden had opened the window. "It's almost eight-thirty; people will be arriving soon."

"Chill, sis, we've got it sorted."

She gave us one final look of disapproval before storming off towards the school entrance.

Well, that was embarrassing. I unbuckled my seatbelt and opened the door before turning back to face Aiden.

"So, was that a better first kiss?" he asked.

For the first time, I sensed insecurity in Aiden's voice. It was only faint but it was definitely there. He had nothing to worry about in that department.

With a satisfied smile, I lifted my hands to smooth his hair to its original style. My face flushed when the realisation that I was the cause of his dishevelled hair finally settled in.

"Definitely," I said with a slight smirk. "I guess I should go to class and learn something for a change."

"I thought you just did learn something," he said jokingly. I smacked him on the hand and scowled. "I'm just playing. Enjoy being a normal teenager. I'll call you when the time is right."

I gave one last smile before slipping out of my seat and watching Aiden disappear around the corner. People had started to arrive so I quietly mixed in with the crowd, making my way to my first class. I could pretend all I liked but I already knew there was no point trying to focus on my classes when mine, Aiden's and the gang's lives were all in jeopardy.

* * *

I sat in my first period Economics class, staring at the whiteboard but not really taking anything in. Even if I didn't have plans to steal the teacher's cars, I still wouldn't have been able to pay attention. I never had the concentration that it took to listen to Mr Cruz's long-winded discussion on income inequality. Mr Cruz was actually one of the best teachers I've had, but Economics had to be the most snore-worthy class in the history of high school courses.

"You see class, income inequality can be easily described as the gap between being rich and being poor," he said, scribbling on the board and waiting patiently for the class to take their notes. "In countries with high levels of income inequality, especially where a significant proportion of the population is below the poverty line, murder, gang violence and theft are relatively high, which really makes us look at how much we rely on money."

I had to clamp my mouth shut to keep from laughing at the mention of theft. My cheeks flared up and Kane looked at me from his seat three desks away. I was going to give myself away if I wasn't more careful. I tried to keep my eyes focused on Mr Cruz, but Kane had shuffled down until he was right next to me.

"Why so red, Nicky?" he smirked as he discretely threw a crumpled ball of paper at Denis while Mr Cruz was facing the board. "Probably locking lips with this one, no doubt."

"Course she was, she can't get enough of me." Denis caught the ball and high-fived Kane.

Romeo turned to me and half smiled before facing his friends. "Come on guys, you know Nic would never lower her standards for a bum like him," he chimed in, laughing at Denis' sullen expression.

"Your mum sure didn't mind lowering her standards for me last night."

Romeo flung a paper ball at him, which soon evolved into a full-on paper ball war.

I shook my head and leaned back into my chair. Mr Cruz was quick to dissolve the fight and we were placed in our groups to prepare for the next exam.

"Sorry about them." Romeo sat down next to me and began scribbling down notes. "I think they've made it their mission to see how far they can push you."

"They've been like that since the eighth grade—it's hardly new."

"True." He frowned. "I think I'm outgrowing all of it."

"Oh? Why's that?"

"I was offered a spot in the gifted program at Herston University," he whispered. "I technically start my university degree next year."

"Let me guess—finance?" I smirked at his nervous laugh.

Six months earlier I had walked in on them using the Economics classroom to organise an illegal betting ring. They were taking bets on almost everything from sporting events to who would get the highest grade in a particular class, and fixing the odds so they would bring in a decent percentage. I suppose they must have been paying attention in Economics class after all.

"You said you wouldn't tell anyone."

"And I haven't," I replied, smiling slightly. "Congratulations on the uni offer, Romeo."

We remained quiet for the rest of the class. I wanted to be excited for him, I really did, but I was too distracted waiting to hear from Aiden. He'd said that he would give me the signal when we needed to meet, but I had no clue when that would be or even *what* it would be. I constantly checked my phone throughout the rest of the class, just in case, but when the bell rang and signalled for the next period I still hadn't heard anything. What was taking him so long?

I packed my bag and left the room to make my way to Legal Studies.

"Hey, wait up."

I turned around and saw Romeo speed walking towards me without his mates. We both had Mrs Collins for Legal Studies, although we never walked there together.

"What's up?" I said, trying to work out what he wanted.

"Are you okay? You seemed really spaced out in class," he said. "You didn't even roast Denis on his incorrect pronunciation of the word 'specific'."

"God, am I really that predictable?"

Romeo laughed at me and put his arm around my shoulder. "Well yes, but that's why we love you," he said. "So what's going on?"

For a second I considered telling him. I don't know why

exactly, but there was a strong voice in my head saying that I could trust him. I wanted to tell him. But there were five of us involved now and it wouldn't be fair for me to put everyone else in jeopardy.

"Nothing really," I sighed. "Just girl stuff."

Girl stuff, really? Well that was an embarrassing attempt at deflection. It must have been enough though, since Romeo opened his mouth to speak, only to close it without a word when we entered our Legal Studies classroom. Thank god for that.

I scanned the room and instantly stiffened when I saw Libby sitting at the back.

"Oh, so that's why you've been off with the fairies," Romeo whispered. "Fight with Libs, huh?"

"Something like that." I caught her gaze as I made my way to my seat in the middle of the room. She tensed and looked down quickly.

I was just about to storm over there and demand that we worked this out, when an unfamiliar voice filled the room.

"Afternoon, class. My name is Mr Peters and I'll be covering today's lesson while Mrs Collins is out sick," he said as he sat down at the teacher's desk at the front of the room. "I don't know what Mrs Collins had planned so I'm just going to get you to read chapter ten of the textbook today. You can work together if you like but keep it strictly schoolwork, thank you."

Oh no. This was bad, really bad. My stomach dropped to the floor and I felt all the blood drain from my face. If Mrs Collins wasn't here that meant her car wasn't either.

Panic started to seep into my mind and my hand shook slightly. Before I could do anything else, I felt my pocket vibrate. I checked that the substitute was distracted before discreetly snaking my hand into my pocket and tapping the message open.

Maths block bathroom. Now. Wait there—Clyde

I read the message three times before it finally clicked. There was no time to message Aiden back. I would have to tell him about Mrs Collins when I saw him.

Raising my hand, I waited for Mr Peters to spot me. When he gestured for me to talk, I asked if I could use the bathroom. The minute he nodded his approval, I shoved my books back into my bag, stood up, and headed for the door.

"Excuse me, sir," I heard Libby say. At first I thought she might say something to make him keep me from leaving since she was still mad. However, it dawned on me that Aiden would have messaged her as well. "Mrs Collins prefers we take a partner whenever we leave the classroom. You know, make sure we're safe."

"Oh?" Mr Peters replied, looking confused, which was to be expected since what Libby had said was a complete lie.

"I can go with Nicole if you like," she said innocently. I couldn't help smiling at her acting skills. "I'm pretty much finished with the chapter anyway."

He'd agree. People always did when Libby wanted something. Nobody was immune to her innocent tone and imploring eyes. Absolutely no one.

He smiled and waved his hand dismissively. While he was preoccupied, I grabbed my bag and slipped it silently across my body. I doubted that we would be coming back today, and since Mr Peters had neglected to mark the roll there was no evidence that any of the class was there, meaning they couldn't prove that we weren't either.

Classic substitute teacher mistake. This was going to be easier than I thought it would be.

I walked out of the room and sped towards the back of the school where the Maths block toilets stood. Why Aiden wanted us there was beyond me.

Entering the girls' bathroom was a mission within itself. It didn't have that putrid smell that always wafted from the boys' toilets, but the moment we walked through the door we were hit with a wall of strong floral smelling perfume and stale cigarette smoke. There were mysterious puddles of water on the floor of the stalls that made it nearly impossible to use the toilet without holding your skirt up to avoid soaking up the strange substance. I really hoped it was water.

Sprawled across the sinks were wads of paper towels that had smudges of make-up and used chewing gum tucked inside, as well as old tampon wrappers in different fluoro colours. There was no denying it: girls are disgusting.

Carefully, I placed my bag underneath the sink. Libby walked in behind me and checked her reflection in the mirror. My heart started to beat more rapidly until the only thing I could hear was the blood rushing behind my ears.

I hated this, I really hated this. I just wanted to fix things. I pursed my lips and narrowed my eyes at Libby. She finally turned to face me and her eyes softened.

"Ready for this?" she asked, as if there was nothing wrong.

"I'm sorry, okay," I blurted, pulling roughly on the loose pieces of my shirt. "I'm sorry that I made you feel like you weren't important. You're my soul sister and no one is more special than that. We started this together and I want to still be together at the end."

"Nic …"

"No, just listen," I interrupted. "I don't want to fight with you. I love you to death, Lib, and you know that. We're family, and family don't act like this. If something went wrong, I'd never forgive myself if we were still …"

I was interrupted by a loud piercing sound that came crashing through the school's intercom.

"What the hell is that?" Libby called out in alarm.

"It's our convenient distraction," I replied, smiling a little with satisfaction despite myself. "That's the evacuation alarm for a bomb scare. I told Aiden to call it in just before we were ready to start. Thank god the school went for it!"

The idea of the distraction was actually created from Libby's ridiculous nickname for our "burning" time in Bellvale Mall. Who knew it would be the perfect inspiration for a bomb scare?

We heard the stampede of students making their way to the school oval where every student and teacher would remain until a bomb squad was called. Whoever came up with that evacuation plan should have re-evaluated their career choice. I'm pretty sure gathering everyone into one location that was easily accessible by the public was a terrible idea. One bomb there could potentially wipe out most of the school population. Good job, board of education. On the other hand, it was a great evacuation plan for anyone who wanted to steal some cars on the other side of the school. I had just bought us at least an hour of privacy.

Without discussion, Libby and I both grabbed our bags and got into the cubicles furthest from the door. Over the echo of footsteps from the nearby hall, I heard Libby's voice coming quietly through the cubicle partition.

"I'm not mad at you, loser," she said. "I'm sorry too. Aiden sort of ripped me a new one earlier, and maybe he had a point. I guess you still love me, even though you probably love Aiden more."

"What makes you think I like Aiden that way?" I asked suspiciously.

"This is high school, Nic," she laughed. "You know that something as juicy as two people making out in the car park would be all over the school in minutes. Everyone knows about you and Aiden."

Oh my god. Kill me now. I cringed and hid my head in my hands. She was right; I was never going to hear the end of this.

"Put me out of my misery!" I joked before turning serious. "Wait, so you're okay with this?"

"Yeah, I'm okay with it, I guess," she said.

A smile broke across my face. She never stopped surprising me. It might not have been the most enthusiastic speech I'd ever heard, but I would have expected her to make me jump through a few hoops before she gave her blessing. Libby was going soft.

"Besides," she added, "he's got a fine arse, so if you weren't going there then I definitely would be."

Never mind, I take that back. She was the same old Libs.

The noise from the hall had died down, so I lowered myself from the toilet and unlatched the lock. I heard Libby do the same thing and we shuffled out just in time to see Aiden and Noah walk into the bathroom.

"Hey, double trouble," Noah said. "I loved the bomb scare ruse. A stroke of criminal genius."

I felt myself blushing a tiny bit at the compliment. "Thanks, Noah."

"Can we escort you ladies to the car park?"

Now it was Libby's turn to blush lightly when Noah held his arm out for her. She took it without a word and they left the room.

"So everything's perfect in paradise again?" Aiden asked, as he saw her smile back at me before leaving.

"I'd say so," I replied flirtatiously. "Apparently a little birdie had a talk with her this morning."

"Is that so?" Aiden said with a raised eyebrow. "Remind me to thank that birdie."

I don't know if all these heists had made me bolder or if it was because I finally knew where I stood with Aiden, but my chest warmed at his subtle flirting. Without hesitating, I walked up next to him and kissed his cheek before lacing my fingers through his.

"No need. I just thanked him for you."

Aiden squeezed my hand lightly and let his smile falter a little. He didn't need to say anything. I knew why his face slipped back into its stony expression and why his eyes returned to their dark state. It was time to steal some cars.

"I'm afraid it's back to business," he sighed. "Ready?"

"As I'll ever be."

He tucked a piece of my hair behind my ear and led the way out of the bathroom, keeping our hands firmly locked together.

14
The Heist

By the time Aiden and I had left the bathroom, Noah and Libby were already waiting for us at the car park. Noah leant against the rusty chain-link fence while Libby stood by his side with a hand on his shoulder. Oh, she had her eye on him all right.

The evacuation alarm continued to ring across the campus and I couldn't see anyone other than our group in the area. At least one thing was going right so far.

"All right, lovebirds," Libby quipped playfully, reaching across and gently poking Aiden in the ribs. "It's about time you two hooked up."

Were we lovebirds now? So that must be what happens when you have a boyfriend. That's if we were even dating. We hadn't had that conversation yet. Although, I think we had a legitimate reason to be distracted. How many other teenagers were dealing with angry Mob bosses and crabby car dealers?

Libby looked at Aiden in disbelief before laughing. He smiled and high-fived Noah, who was so excited that he reminded me of a small puppy. I highly doubted that he would ever grow bored of all the drama.

Seeing everyone finally relax was nice, even if it was only for a moment. But, almost as if I had said it aloud, everyone suddenly remembered what we were here for and what we had been through and their cheery moods sobered.

"I hate to break up the fun, guys, but we do have a heist to get through," Noah spoke up. "Care to carry on, Aiden?"

"Right, well, you all know the basics. We each take a car

and do our own dirty work," Aiden explained, his eyes shifting back into their darker state. "Someone will have to stay behind to keep watch and let us know if it's safe to come and collect the remaining cars."

"I'll do it," I volunteered almost immediately. I knew someone was going to have to stay behind, and logically it had to be me. Noah had been working alongside Aiden for years and regardless of how involved I'd been in the previous heists, Libby still had the faster hands. My talents were stronger in the planning stage, so I was fine being the lookout.

"Okay," Aiden replied, tightening his grip on my shoulder. "Hang on, where's Sash?"

I hadn't noticed that Sasha wasn't there, although the lack of snippy comments should have been a dead giveaway. I should have seen this coming.

Everyone remained silent until Aiden yanked his arm from around me and squeezed his hands into tight fists.

"Are you bloody kidding me?" he exclaimed, anger flaring in his hazel eyes. "She's seriously doing this again after everything that happened last time?"

This was the first time I saw Aiden lose his temper since Bobby and his thugs confronted us. He paced erratically and no one knew what to do. We didn't have time for this.

I don't know what possessed me but before I could really register what I was doing, I had stepped in front of him and laced my arms around his waist. Touching someone, especially Aiden, was still a new concept to me and yet it didn't make me feel uncomfortable. His heart was beating fast and I squeezed tighter until I felt the tension in his body loosen.

"There's nothing we can do about it right now," I soothed. "We have bigger issues to worry about."

"Speaking of which," Libby cut in. "We haven't mentioned Mrs Collins yet."

Aiden frowned and looked down to face me, waiting for my reply.

"Mrs Collins is out sick today," I revealed, loosening my grip on him. "This means we're down a car."

The look on Aiden's face was enough to make my chest tighten. His eyes turned black and his eyebrows knitted together in frustration. Running a hand through his hair, he asked Noah to search the car park.

Wait, what? I frowned as Noah walked off and started looking over each of the parked cars. "What is he doing?"

"He's more than just a tech guy," Aiden replied. "He's got Dom's list pretty much memorised so he's finding us a replacement."

"Well, aren't we full of surprises?" Libby remarked, watching Noah's backside as he bent down to look at another car.

Good to know all the stress from the past few days hadn't killed her hormones. Honestly, did she even realise the predicament we were in? Sasha wasn't here and we had wasted way too much time already. We needed to get moving and soon.

Noah returned and started to talk but an insistent buzzing from my pocket distracted me. I slid my phone out and raised an eyebrow in surprise at the text message:

Nic, where R U? Class was evacuated 4 alarm— Romeo.

Typical Romeo. Of course he'd worry about a missing classmate. Without replying, I lowered my phone and tried to put my focus back on the plan instead. Even if I knew what to say, I couldn't reply to Romeo without giving something away.

"What do you mean we can't?" Libby's voice caught my attention.

I had missed what they were talking about, but their faces

were tense and they looked like they were gearing up for a fight. This couldn't be good.

"What's the matter?"

Aiden caught my gaze and exhaled loudly. "Noah thinks we won't be able to do the two trips."

"I don't think it, I know it," he corrected. "Dom's is a twenty-minute drive from here and we've already wasted fifteen minutes. There's no way to complete two trips without risking someone spotting us."

He was right. There just wasn't enough time and we weren't going to risk all of us getting caught.

I started tracing small circles on Aiden's hand to try and calm him down but it was pretty much pointless. His jaw was clenched to the point that he'd need to see a dentist if he didn't chill out.

"Could we take what we can from here and do another heist elsewhere?" Libby added, shrugging.

That wouldn't work. Once the final bell rang and the teachers discovered their cars were missing, the police would be notified and everyone would be on high alert. Noah suggested making a deal with Dom but Aiden was quick to dismiss that idea. If anyone knew how bad deals with Dom could go, it was him.

Time was running out and we still had no idea what to do.

My palms became moist and I was about to wipe them when my phone buzzed again. Looking down, I saw that Romeo had sent me another message to ask if I was okay. I had an idea but it was a crazy one. The others were definitely going to hate it.

Without glancing up, I quickly typed a message to Romeo telling him where we were and to meet me right now, with Denis and Kane, making sure no one saw them.

I couldn't be sure exactly why I thought Romeo and his friends would be the best option, I didn't even trust them that much. All I knew was that we needed extra people.

I slipped my phone back into my pocket just as Noah started rattling off our odds of success.

"So did you find a replacement?" Aiden asked, drawing his attention from the time situation.

"I found another car, but you're not going to like it," he said, pointing to a Ford Thunderbird parked in a reserved car space. "Principal Martinez's car is the closest fit."

Oh god. This was hilarious. It was like everything that could go wrong was going wrong and all I could do was laugh at the mess we were in. I mean come on, what was next? A flat tyre?

"Well, I'm glad one of us finds this funny," Aiden said, pulling me a closer. "But there's still the issue of not enough time."

"I may have fixed that."

Denis rounded the corner, making an obnoxious bird noise with Kane close behind him, smirking and clapping his mate on the back. Romeo seemed more reserved, shaking his head at them and waving at us.

"What did you do?" Aiden whispered harshly.

I expected him to be upset but I didn't think he would be this angry. He removed his hands from my waist within a second and the others all stared at me like they were seeing me for the first time.

"Look, I know it's nuts but we need more people, simple as that," I argued, holding my hands out.

The boys came up and greeted each of us with their usual jokes. Denis's flirting earned him a glare from both Noah and Aiden, whose hand had protectively snaked back around my waist.

"So are ya going to tell us why you dragged us away from such a thrilling drill?" Kane asked.

"You're going to help us steal a few of the cars here."

Ripping off the Band-Aid was the best approach.

Kane and Denis's smiles slipped straight off their faces and their eyebrows shot up in surprise. Romeo looked like he was waiting for someone to come out and tell him that he had just been punked.

"What makes you think we'd ever do a thing like that?" Denis frowned and squared his shoulders. "We should report you before you do something stupid."

If only he knew what we had already done.

"You won't be reporting us." My voice was low and icy. "And you will be joining us if you don't want everyone to find out about your little betting ring."

The boys glared at me in disbelief. If one word of the betting ring got out they'd be looking at suspension, possibly expulsion.

"You wouldn't," Romeo replied.

"I would." They didn't know just how desperate we were. "You think any college would take you with that on your permanent record? You might as well say goodbye to business school and hello to flipping burgers for minimum wage for the rest of your life."

Libby made a choking noise and looked at me in shock. I hadn't mentioned the betting ring to her before so I'm sure she'd have a few things to say about that later. Aiden was looking at me like it was the first time he'd ever seen me.

I guess it almost was. The old me wouldn't have even been involved in this, let alone blackmail others into it. Pretty ironic, when you think about it. But I wanted my life back and if that meant making a threat or two then so be it.

"Fine," Romeo spoke up after a few minutes of silence. "We help you and you forget everything you know about the ring, agreed?"

Looks like I wasn't the only one who could harden up when needed. I don't think I had ever seen Romeo look so tense before. I exhaled the breath I had been holding and nodded.

"Agreed. Now we need to hurry if we're ever going to make it out of here."

With a nod of his head, Aiden slipped out of my grasp and took off towards the Chevy Impala. Once everyone had picked their targets, it became obvious that we were still one person short. Even if I went with the first lot, we still had only seven people for eight cars.

Our only option was to have someone come back and help me take the last two cars. Aiden volunteered immediately. It was dangerous but we seemed to be the leaders now and it was our responsibility. We also knew how to keep our mouths shut.

The others had their cars sorted; Noah helped the boys while I helped Libby. I still wasn't too great with a jimmy, so Libby tripped the lock and opened the dashboard panel. I took over on the wires because Libby found them confusing. But even with Noah's lessons and Aiden's tips, I still had to concentrate to find the right ones.

"What the hell was the deal with the betting ring?" Libby hissed suddenly.

"What about it?" I said irritably. My fingertips were sweating from the tension, making it hard to hold the wires still.

"Well, I just have one or two questions," she replied, dripping sarcasm. "Little things like, when did you find out about it, when were you going to tell me, and where do you get off threatening our friends?"

I brushed my hair out of my eyes and looked at her. There was a really nasty reply bubbling, and I should have swallowed it down, but I was too stressed.

"So you have a problem with people blackmailing their friends, do you? Like, say, threatening to destroy their chances of getting into their perfect university? Or getting them involved with crime, like shoplifting, maybe, or car stealing?"

I could see I had hit home. There was guilt in her eyes,

though she was trying not to show it. I should have left it there, but I couldn't resist one last dig.

"I'm just doing what I have to do to get us out of this, but you're the one who got us into it. This is your fault, Libby. Your fault. Never forget that."

I twisted the wires together and the engine jumped into life. Libby looked like she was going to cry. I felt like a monster, but it was too late to unsay those things now. Instead I slid out of the car and jogged over to Aiden, wrapping my arms around him as if that could make everything all right.

No one told me how addictive being affectionate with someone could be. Or maybe it was just Aiden's scent of vanilla and leather.

"Stay hidden and be careful. I'm still worried about Sasha, I can't handle worrying about you as well," he said, circling his arms tight around me. "I'll be back before you know it."

"Promise?" I asked, refusing to loosen my hold until I had an answer.

"Of course," Aiden replied, brushing a hand through my hair. "Then I'm going to take you on an actual date. We seemed to have skipped that part." He leant forward and pressed his warm lips to mine. No matter how often we kissed, I doubted I'd ever get used to Aiden's mouth.

Everything seemed normal when it was just the two of us. I didn't feel like I was a monster or that there was any darkness. I just felt like myself. It made me forget everything, even the fact that we were supposed to be in the middle of Silverlake's biggest car heist.

The sound of an approaching car broke my trance and I separated from him to see the others lined up in each of their cars, ready to go.

"Come on, lover boy," Noah called out. The other boys idled behind him, quiet and sullen. "You can suck face with Nic once we're done."

Aiden unravelled himself from my body, ran over to his vehicle and closed the door just as Noah headed out of the car park, followed by the others.

I waved at Aiden as he left, giving him a wink. The car park was suddenly quiet and there was no one around to keep me from thinking about what was going to happen when we finally saw Bobby again.

In the privacy of the empty lot, I let my face crumble.

* * *

Time ticked by slowly and although it had only been ten minutes, it felt like days since the group had left. I tried to stay hidden as much as the building would allow, but I couldn't stop myself from pacing. Before I only had to worry what happened to me and Libby, but now Aiden was an important part of my life. I bit my nails as I paced, lost in my own thoughts.

"Hello, Nicole," came a silky female voice.

I whipped around and saw Sasha standing a few steps away from me with her hands loosely crossed against her chest.

"Sasha?" I questioned dumbly. "Where the hell have you been?"

I narrowed my eyes at her when she grinned. How could she find this amusing? I was starting to think my initial feelings towards her were correct. She just didn't seem to care about any of this.

"I've been a little busy actually," she replied nonchalantly. "I see you and my brother are close?"

Was she being serious? She wanted to discuss my relationship status with her brother after disappearing for most of the day? She knew how important this heist was.

I drew my body up until my back was straight and gave her the best bitch face I could muster. "That's correct."

She eyed me for a moment before cocking an eyebrow and smirking. "That's a real shame," she sneered. "We can't have that getting back to Bobby now, can we?"

The air flew out of my lungs—Sasha had just confirmed that she was connected to Bobby. Her eyes grew colder and a satisfied smile spread across her face. I dropped my gaze to her hands, which had slipped into her pocket. Anger flooded my body and I moved my hand to grab my phone and contact Aiden.

"Nah uh," Sasha mocked, pulling a slim metal object from her pocket. "Now, I know you know what this is. Don't make me use it."

Squinting slightly, my mouth popped open a fraction when I saw the familiar gun. She raised it up until it was level with my chest. My heart thumped with adrenaline and I fought to keep my hands steady. Strangely, despite the shakes, I didn't feel fear like I thought I would. I only felt numb, and somewhat curious.

"Why?" I asked, trying to connect the dots.

"Family business, of course," she replied as if it were the most obvious thing on the planet. "Dad's wanted us to join him since we were old enough to know what cars were."

Dad? Oh god. It started to make sense. Bobby should have killed us the moment he had us cornered. No one ever lived after a run in with the Zangari family.

Wait a minute, if Sasha was Bobby's daughter then that could only mean one thing. Aiden was related to Bobby as well.

What the hell had I done? My stomach was sinking so fast that any minute I was going to throw up. I trusted him and he lied to me. Brooke had died and we still didn't know exactly how badly Greg was injured, all because Sasha and Aiden wanted to steal a few Porsches. Their own father's Porsches.

"Why would you tell Aiden to use the Porsches to settle his debt with Dom? You knew they were your dad's."

Sasha's grin deepened even more and a flicker of delight went through her eyes. "I thought it would have been obvious," she smirked, lowering the gun a little as she spoke. "I wanted my brother to join me."

What kind of messed up logic was that? Stealing from Bobby only made things worse, not better. I was so beyond confused that I was going to need a translator just to work this all out.

"Why not just ask him like a normal person?" I spat. "Why drag us all into your family drama?"

She dropped her smirk and narrowed her eyes. I knew I was asking too many questions but my curiosity was eating at me. I also needed to keep her distracted until Aiden returned.

A pang of doubt shot through my body at the thought of Aiden. He loved his sister more than anything else, even if he didn't show it. I wasn't sure whether he'd even choose my side once he knew what Sasha's plan was.

"You may think you know Aiden better than me, but you don't," she answered. "He may be a little dark but he's still a decent person. There was no way he'd go for Dad's crew if I just asked him. That's why I set up Aiden with the Porsches."

I wrinkled my face and tried to understand what she was saying over the loud thump of my heart.

Sasha sighed. "Aiden's good at stealing cars." She tapped her foot impatiently. "Dad saw that, but Aiden refused to join us. Except he wouldn't have had a choice once Dad caught him stealing from the family. But then you came along and screwed it all up."

She practically spat the last few words out, tightening her grip on the gun. My stomach twisted tightly and I swallowed hard.

"I didn't ask to be a part of this," I replied, shifting a few steps away from her. "I'm sure you can remember."

"It doesn't matter what you wanted. Aiden brought you into

this and I'm not okay with that," she snapped, anger flashing in her eyes. "I tried to get rid of you before but Brooke got in the way."

This time there was no confusion. I knew exactly what she was getting at and it made my body grow clammy. Brooke wasn't supposed to die, I was.

"It was you," I said timidly. I don't know why I felt the urge to ask but I couldn't help myself.

"Brooke's death was unfortunate," Sasha replied with no remorse. "No matter, it's time to correct my mistakes."

She'd already pointed the gun to my head by the time I fully understood what she meant. Whatever fear I thought I had suppressed was back and I began to take shallow breaths, trying not to hyperventilate.

I pulled to the left, attempting to dodge the gun's path. There was no looking past this. Sasha was going to kill me and I wasn't going to see how it all turned out.

She squeezed the trigger and I jumped back, waiting for the bullet to hit me. I flinched when I heard the gun blast but I felt no pain. In fact I felt nothing except the wind circling around us. I opened my eyes and saw Sasha slouched against Aiden, who was holding her around the waist.

"Wait, where, huh?" I stammered, still a little shocked.

"I got back a few minutes ago." He was gazing down at Sasha with a look void of any emotion. "I just reacted. I saw her with a gun and I did the first thing that came to mind."

I looked back at Sasha and noticed the blood trickling from her head. There was a small gash to the right side of her temple and dirt was clinging to the dark centre. She wasn't moving but her chest still rose and fell as she breathed.

Aiden hadn't shot her if the large misshapen rock still clutched tightly in his hand was any indication. He had hit her in the head, though. I don't know which was worse.

Sasha's gun lay on the ground between us. It must have gone off when Aiden struck her. How close was the bullet from hitting me? More importantly, how close was I to joining Brooke?

Aiden hadn't moved from where he was standing with Sasha. I waited for his explanation, his excuses. Anything really, but he remained silent.

"We should probably get going, Dom's waiting."

Oh great, dark Aiden was back. His posture was once again tense and his shoulders squared. His expression was the same one he wore when he didn't want to be questioned.

Too bad. I was so angry that it wasn't going to work on me this time.

"Is it true then? Bobby's your dad?"

"Yes."

"Why the hell did you lie to me?"

"I didn't lie, I just omitted the truth."

He could not be serious right now. This was a betrayal of ridiculous proportions. We did all of this for a stupid family feud? Are you kidding me? Brooke and Greg would still be around if it weren't for them. I wouldn't be blackmailing, stealing and lying to everyone if they had just handled their crap in private.

It wouldn't have been wise to keep waiting for Aiden to agree that he had lied. He was as stubborn as Libby was when she wanted something. I just needed to know one thing.

"Did you know the cars belonged to Bobby?"

He looked at me briefly before answering. "Not until we went back to check on Brooke." He relaxed his shoulders slightly. "The rest was pretty easy to work out after that. I just didn't think she'd do that to me."

Seriously? Because I thought it was something she'd do without hesitation. But then again, she wasn't my sister.

I pushed Aiden a little more for answers but kind of wish I hadn't. He didn't want to work with Bobby because he didn't want to deal with the expectations that the rest of the family would have of him. He wanted to be his own leader with his own crew.

"Dad doesn't hesitate to kill those who disrespect him or his business," Aiden explained. "He'd expect the same of me and I'm not interested in that. I might use force sometimes but I'm not a murderer."

The sincerity in his eyes was overwhelming. Obviously he didn't want any of this to happen, but it had. I could get over his manipulation and deceit when it came to getting me here and I could work towards getting over the fact that he lied to me once again, but I didn't know if I could get past this.

He was Bobby Zangari's son and that was a massive deal. It would be almost impossible to trust him. The Zangaris were manipulative, violent thugs and it was obvious that Aiden held some of those same traits. How could he not? He was raised by thugs after all.

I was still so angry with him but we just didn't have time for this right now and Aiden obviously knew that as well since he kept peering around to see if anyone was coming towards the car park. This would have to wait.

"Well, I hope it was worth it." A small trickle of satisfaction ran through me when I saw him flinch at the bite in my tone. I wasn't ready to let it go just yet. "Let's not keep Dom waiting."

"I'll be there soon," he replied, dragging his sister to rest against the car park fence. "I need to talk to her and make sure an ambulance gets here first."

I opened my mouth to protest but Aiden cut in quickly.

"I have to, Nic," he urged. "She's my sister."

There was no way to argue with that. Regardless of the stunt she pulled, she was still his family and I was too upset to really say any different. I just needed to put some distance between us. Fast.

I passed him and walked over to the two remaining cars on our list. Mr Peterson, the clueless 10th grade English teacher, had left his door unlocked. This time around, I was able to hot-wire the car without too much difficulty and felt the engine purr.

With one last deep breath, I slipped out of the car spot and passed Aiden as he stood over his sister. My hands still shook from having the gun in my face and I wanted nothing more than to cry until I had no more tears left. Instead, I turned right at the car park exit and drove to Dom's, trying my hardest not to think about Aiden and whether he was going to make it back to the garage.

15
Bobby/Goodbye

Dom walked out of her office as I drove through the warehouse's darkened back entrance. My hands still shook slightly from my encounter with Sasha but the throb in my head was silencing any thoughts on that.

The whole time I was driving to Dom's, I couldn't stop thinking about how Aiden was Bobby's son and that he didn't tell me. Sasha had hoped this would show Aiden that he should join her and the Mob, and I didn't know for sure that he'd never do it. He could easily slip right into place with them and forget all about being the Aiden that I loved.

Except he didn't. It would have been so easy for him to accept Sasha's proposal, but he chose not to. He knocked out his own sister for me.

Aiden was more than just the lies he told. Yeah, I could stay mad, but what was the point of it all? Nothing was going to change what had already happened. He had no say in who his family was, and I couldn't exactly say that I would be upfront about it either if I was in his position.

A sharp knock on the car window pulled me back to where I was. Aiden looked worn out and the usual cocky gleam in his eyes had been replaced with an exhausted and raw expression. His smile was the only comforting thing about him at that moment.

Relief was all I felt. I didn't realise how nervous I was about him staying with Sasha until I saw him here.

He chose us. I smiled at the realisation and flung my door open, colliding with him in a desperate hug. God, I'd never get enough of his vanilla aftershave and the smell that was just simply him.

"Someone missed me," he teased, holding me tighter around the waist.

"Shut up and let me have my moment," I retorted, smiling into his shoulder. We remained glued to each other for as long as we could before we needed to detach enough to talk.

"You okay?" I asked, looking him over to check for any injuries, although I knew most of the damage couldn't be seen on the outside. I may not have known Sasha for long but I did know enough to see that she meant a lot to Aiden.

"I can't really answer that," he replied, resting his forehead against mine. "My own sister set me up. I'm always going to love her, but I just don't know how I should feel about that."

Poor Aiden. The closest I had to a sibling was Libby and I don't know if I'd be able to cope if she did what Sasha had. He was handling this in the best way he could.

I lifted my head from his and placed my hands on either side of his cheeks. "It's okay not to know," I said softly.

Sometimes I think he forgot that no one could ever possibly know how to feel in all situations. He didn't need to have all the answers. I wrapped my arms around his neck and dragged him back into a tight hug, laying a quick kiss on his neck.

"If you guys looked any more like something out of a romantic drama then I'd have to stock up on popcorn and tissues," Dom quipped, jutting her hip out and looking at us with a disgusted look.

"Oh please," Aiden scoffed. "The number of times I've walked in on you and Jill being all cute, I could have stopped watching TV altogether."

Dom's jaw tightened and her eyes briefly showed embarrassment before annoyance overtook them. "Whatever," she said. "Have you got my keys or what?"

"I believe these are yours," I said, throwing the keys into her outstretched hand.

"Good," she replied, curling her hands around them. "The Porsches are in the garage and the keys are in the cabinet. Take them and go." Without saying anything else, Dom marched back to her office and slammed the door.

I rolled my shoulders and sighed inwardly when I heard a small pop. I still needed to prepare myself for what was left to do. We were halfway through this nightmare and now the hardest part of all was coming up. We still had to face Bobby.

"I'm going to grab the keys and then we can head off," Aiden said, bringing my attention back to the warehouse. "Go check on the others and I'll be back soon."

I nodded and walked out to the side building that held the break room. Aiden had pointed it out when we first came here and I could hear light chatter coming from inside. Walking in, I saw that everyone had remained after bringing their cars in, even Romeo and his mates. Their faces all held a different emotion that under other circumstances would have been comical. Some were scared, some were pumped and some were just plain bored.

"Nic!" Libby said. "What took you so long? Where's Aiden?"

God, it was good to see her. Even though I had said some very mean things to Libby, I still felt so much love for her. I pulled her into a quick hug. Her embrace made me feel safe, which wasn't really something that I was feeling a lot of lately. In fact, I couldn't even remember the last time I felt remotely safe without the embrace of another. So much for independence.

"We had a bit of an issue, but we're here now," I answered, trying to keep my face even. The drama with Sasha wasn't something that I had any business sharing. If Aiden wanted everyone to know then he would have to be the one to tell them. "Aiden's just picking up the keys for the Porsches."

"Wait," Noah said. "So you're going to see Bobby now?"

"We sure are," Aiden replied as he entered the room. He threw an arm around me. "You ready?"

I nodded and took the keys he held out.

"Hang on," Noah said, bringing us to a halt. "Why don't we go with you?"

Aiden shifted in his spot and gripped the keys a little tighter. "Bobby hasn't seen you guys yet," he said. "I don't want him to know who else was involved with the heist. This is just easier."

I'm sure that wasn't the only reason he didn't want them there. I mean, how would he even begin to explain the family connection?

Noah bit down on his lip but didn't protest. He was Aiden's best friend and they had been through a lot together, after all.

And I could see Aiden's reasoning. I wouldn't want Libby anywhere near Bobby if I could help it. Bobby was too much like a labyrinth: once you entered his world, you'd be lucky to find your way out unscathed.

"Well, we better go," I said, after the silence became a little uncomfortable. "Libs, I'll see you at home later. Stay safe everyone."

After saying a quick goodbye, Aiden led the way to the garage where the Porsches sat waiting for us.

"I thought you could take the purple one," Aiden said with a smirk. "I know how fond you are of the colour."

"Always the gentleman."

Once inside, I let the smile slip from my face. I know Aiden was acting all carefree for my benefit, but it was pointless. We both knew how serious this meeting was going to be. We just didn't have the nerve to admit it out loud.

I slipped the key into the ignition and started the engine with a roar. Taking one final deep breath, I pulled out of the warehouse and led the way to Fairview Drive.

* * *

Turning into the cluster of streets, I arrived a few moments before Aiden. He couldn't have been that far behind me so I parked out front of the familiar buildings and cut the engine.

Dom was bad enough; now we had to settle our deal with Bobby and time was ticking. I had no idea how we were supposed to contact him to let him know we had arrived or what we were going to say.

I was an idiot of course. Aiden would know exactly how to contact his dad. I may have forgiven the fact that Aiden kept that connection a secret, but it was still hard to comprehend. I had also seriously underestimated Silverlake and the crazy networks of illegal activity going on just beneath the surface.

After a few more deep breaths, I slowly opened the driver's car door and carefully got out just in time to see Aiden drive up and park on the other side of me.

"It's show time," he said, walking over and putting his hand on the small of my back. "You ready?"

I nodded and leaned into him, placing my hand around his waist. A wave of relief surged through me. This entire mess was almost over and soon we would be able to breathe freely without worrying about Bobby or Dom.

One thing was for sure, this was the last time I was ever going to steal a car.

Aiden reached into his pocket and pulled out his phone. Watching the ease with which Aiden spoke to Bobby, I began to feel nauseous.

Crap. I must have made it too clear what I was thinking because Aiden suddenly looked upset.

"I'm sorry," I said.

"Don't be," he replied, tightening his grip on me. "It's not like I've given you any reason to trust me."

"I do trust you."

"I know you do to a degree, but not completely," he continued as I lowered my gaze. "I have a lot to make up for and believe me when I say that I'll keep trying until you're able to trust me wholeheartedly. You deserve that much."

He gripped my chin softly and angled my head up until I was looking at him again. He half smiled and pulled me closer until his lips had enclosed over mine. It was a quick kiss, but I could feel his remorse and determination. I knew we were going to be okay regardless of how long it took us.

"How cute," I heard a rough, sarcastic voice say. "Just warms my heart, really."

We broke apart in a flash and turned to see Frank a short distance from us with his arms crossed over himself and a sneer on his face. Bobby and Tommy were a step behind him, amusement showing on their faces.

"Come on, Frank," Bobby said, walking in front of him. "Young love is refreshing."

Aiden visibly stiffened from the familiar voice, stepping closer to Bobby and holding the newly cut keys for both Porsches.

"Here you are," he said. "We took the liberty of making a set of keys since we originally went without them." Aiden emphasised the last few words with so much venom that I was sure people all the way over in America flinched. There was some serious fury brewing in his eyes and it was becoming obvious that we needed to end this family reunion. Right now.

"Well, aren't we in a hurry today?" Bobby said, tossing the keys to Frank. "Take the cars back to my house and wait there. I have a few things to sort out with these two."

"But boss—" Tommy started to argue.

"Go," he replied more forcibly. "I'll be fine here for a few minutes without you."

Both men seemed like they wanted to argue more, but one

glare from Bobby silenced them and they left quickly.

"I trust that they are in perfect condition?" Bobby asked.

"Of course," I replied, clearing my throat when it came out groggily. "They're exactly as they were when we took them."

Bobby's eyes locked with mine and he refused to break our connection even as Tommy and Frank revved the Porsche engines and took off down the street.

What the hell was going on? He had what he wanted, so why wasn't he leaving? That sickly, sinking feeling entered my stomach and I just knew I was missing something. I should have known that Bobby Zangari wasn't going to make this simple. Not even for his own blood.

"What's going on?" I finally asked aloud once I saw Aiden stiffen next to me.

"There's a catch," Aiden said. "Isn't there, Father dearest?"

"Correct," Bobby replied in a bored tone, ignoring the bite in Aiden's voice. "You didn't think that returning these cars would be it? I've let you play *child* long enough, Aiden."

What was that supposed to mean? This wasn't going the way it was supposed to at all, and this time my brain was not offering any solutions.

Looking between the two men, I shifted my weight from one foot to the other. Bobby had the same eyes as Aiden, so it wasn't too hard to notice the familiar glint that appeared when a bad idea was about to form.

"I'm assuming you have something in mind then?" Aiden questioned bitterly.

This power play was terrifying. Aiden was playing Russian roulette right now and I was going to be the collateral damage. Sure, it was fine for him to be explosive with his dad, but Bobby the Mob leader had no reason to leave me alive.

"It's time to grow up and come to work for me," Bobby said coolly. "In fact, I want both of you to work for me."

A moment passed where the world seemed to freeze in place and all noise was sucked out of the air. It took me a second for my mind to catch up.

"Wait, what?"

"He wants us to join the Mob," Aiden clarified, clenching his fists. "Dad's wanted me by his side for years and I'm assuming he wants you too after seeing what you can do."

I looked at Aiden and noticed his expression harden. "I don't understand."

"What don't you understand, sweetheart?" Bobby said. I cringed at the nickname. "You will work for me or I will kill you. Pretty simple."

Before I could reply, Aiden strode over until he was only inches from Bobby. "This is crap," he spat. "You can't do that."

"Oh, can't I?" Bobby hissed, rustling around in his coat pocket and pulling out a sleek metal handgun and holding it up to Aiden's head.

If Aiden was afraid, he didn't show it. He continued to glare at Bobby with intense hatred. Bobby pulled back the hammer and pushed the gun a little harder into Aiden's forehead. Aiden jutted up his jaw, daring Bobby to pull the trigger.

"Or maybe I'm going about this all wrong." Bobby's eyes sparkled dangerously as his lips curled into a light smirk. "I could just put your little mutt girlfriend down and then maybe you won't be so distracted."

The terror I had felt with Sasha was nothing compared to the moment Bobby shifted the gun from Aiden's temple to point right between my eyes.

This was it. Our game of Russian roulette was over and I had lost.

I was so stupid. All I wanted was to keep my head down and get the hell out of Silverlake the minute graduation was over. Actually, I probably would have just skipped the damn graduation altogether. But none of that was going to happen now. I was only going to leave Silverlake in a body bag and as much as I wish I could, I had no one else to blame but myself.

I barely had enough time to inhale sharply before Aiden smacked the gun out of Bobby's hand and shoved him away. There was no hesitation on Bobby's end. He lunged at Aiden and started to punch him in the jaw repeatedly.

Screaming and dust. That was all I could comprehend in that moment. I didn't even realise that I was the one who was screaming until my throat began to ache. The sound of flesh beating into more flesh made my body tremble violently and my throat close up.

There was nothing I could do. No matter how much I screamed and begged Bobby to stop, he continued to throw his fist into Aiden's face, not even phased by the blood that was staining his hands.

"Stop, please stop!"

I tried to pull his hand away but he was too strong. My heart beat so loudly I couldn't hear anything but the sickening rhythmic sound of Bobby's grunts of exertion and Aiden's small gasps for air.

Wait, why was he gasping for air? I stopped trying to pull Bobby off Aiden when I saw something that almost stopped my heart altogether. Bobby had his beefy hands wrapped tightly around Aiden's neck and was squeezing with so much strength that his knuckles were white and Aiden's face was pale.

"Stop, please, you're killing him! Please!"

He wasn't stopping. Why wasn't he stopping? Oh god. My eyes started to sting with tears and I stumbled backwards, falling to the ground.

Aiden wasn't kicking his feet out anymore and his hands fell from where they were once pulling on Bobby's.

He was dying.

I needed to get help or move or, I don't know, do something. I stumbled back and fell to the ground. I was prepared to run to the nearest person and beg for their help when my hand bumped against something cold.

Bobby's gun.

Without even thinking about it, I curled my hand around the weapon and pulled it close. It was heavier than I thought it would have been.

"Da—" Aiden's voice was nothing but a strained grunt.

That was it. There was no more time. Without another thought, I raised the gun and pulled the trigger.

Silence. Someone had flipped the switch and muted everything around us. The only sound I could hear was the ringing in my ears. My hands vibrated from the force of the bullet and my fingers felt like I had stuck them in ice long enough for my nerve endings to burn off. Bobby lay slumped on top of Aiden and neither was moving.

Crap, what if I had shot Aiden? Oh god. I actually shot someone.

"Aiden?"

I was too afraid to approach them. I was terrified because I had fired the bullet that was causing the ground to clump into little patches of dirty blood. But I was simultaneously underwhelmed at having fired that bullet as simply as if I were clicking on a ballpoint pen. There was no hesitation, just action.

The sound of spluttering made my head snap back towards the two men. For a second, I thought that Bobby was picking himself up, but that thought was quickly dismissed when I saw Aiden pushing him to the side.

I was so damn happy to see him sitting up. Every breath he took was like a wave of relief smacking me fair in the face. He was alive.

I ran over to him and grabbed his arm while he rubbed his

neck tenderly. Thick red marks across his jugular were slowly darkening.

Chancing a glance at Bobby, my stomach clenched at the hole in the side of his head. I'd killed him. I had actually ended someone else's life. What the hell did I do?

"Come on." Aiden's voice broke through my panic. "We need to get out of here before his men come looking for him.

"But—"

"We can't be here when they come back, trust me."

His face was void of emotion as he lifted himself up gingerly and leant against me. We walked to the end of the street in almost silence, only broken when Aiden called for a lift. It felt strange to be doing something as normal as going home after everything we had been through.

* * *

By the time we had walked far enough away for it to be safe for a taxi to pick us up, a couple hours had passed since the heist. My heart was still pounding from our encounter with Bobby. I hadn't checked whether he was still breathing but he had a hole in his head big enough for me to see inside, so that was enough for me.

I had killed someone. The very thought of it made me want to throw up or cry. Or maybe both. The more we tried to get ourselves out of trouble, the further damage we did.

"Ready to go in?" Aiden rested his hand over mine.

I tried to stop them from trembling as Aiden paid the taxi driver. "As ready as I'll ever be."

Opening the door, I started walking towards the house and noticed that Aiden's car was parked crookedly on the driveway.

"Libby must have brought it back for you," I said, turning around to see Aiden pulling out his spare set of keys.

"Want to come in?" With all the drama of the day, I hadn't really had a chance to talk to him about the kiss in the car and what it all meant.

God, I was a horrible person. I shot someone and all I could think about was my relationship status. But what was I supposed to do? I just wanted to be able to fix something. I needed to have some kind of control and the only way I was going to get myself together was by focusing on the things that I could change.

I killed Bobby and I needed to accept that before my mind destroyed me. So that was just what I was going to do. Bobby was in the past and Aiden was a part of my future. Simple as that.

"What about your parents?" Aiden asked, swinging the keys between his fingers. "Won't they be concerned if you bring a boy in the house?"

"Is bad boy Aiden scared of two harmless parents?" I teased, coming closer to him. "Besides, they're still at work." I placed a hand on his bicep and slowly slid it down until I was lacing my fingers through his.

"How could I say no to you?" he said, pocketing his keys and keeping hold of my hand.

I bit my lip and pulled him across the yard and through the front door. I could make this work. With every teasing touch, flirty look and sassy remark, things would feel normal.

We just needed a little time.

I couldn't hear Libby but I knew she had to be there. Aiden came up behind me and twisted his hand until he was wrapped around me. I pulled him closer and inhaled his familiar leather and vanilla scent. I could definitely get used to this.

"Honey, we're home," Aiden called out. I laughed hollowly.

Without warning, Libby came barrelling down the stairs and thrust a giant black suitcase into my hands, pushing us towards the front door. Either she was on some serious drugs or something was going on.

My smile quickly dissipated at the thought. What now?

"You have to go," she screeched. "You and Aiden need to leave *right now*."

Okay, something was really, really wrong. There was a panic in her eyes that I had never seen before. Oh god. Maybe this was about Bobby. If she knew then that meant everyone else knew. Or it meant that Bobby was still alive. Either way, I was royally screwed.

She kept pushing us until we were out the front door. The panicked look remained etched on her face.

"Would you stop pushing for two seconds?" I asked, giving her a quick shake. "What's going on?"

She swallowed quickly and took a deep breath to calm her shaking hands. "The police are on their way," she said a little more calmly. "Apparently someone saw you and Aiden taking the last two cars and the police are coming to arrest you both."

I was not expecting that. How could I forget about the damn car heist? Sure, Bobby's death definitely overshadowed that but we still committed a serious offence at Sterling High. When did my life become such a mess?

My stomach did a queasy somersault and I felt the blood rush from my face so quickly that I was sure I would resemble a ghost soon enough. This couldn't be happening, not after everything we'd just gone through.

"What about you and the others?"

"We were gone before the witness showed up," she stammered. "I doubt the cops think that you two did it on your own but without evidence, they can't do anything to us."

"Hang on," Aiden cut in. "How do you know the cops are coming?"

Libby turned his way and flashed her phone at him.

"Noah and I thought we'd listen to the police scanner when we were done to see when the teachers noticed their cars were gone," she replied. "We heard your names mentioned and that they were coming to bring you in for questioning. They said they had witnesses that confirmed your identities."

This was it. Our streak was over and we were going to have to face what we did. Game over, checkmate, the end. Whatever you wanted to call it, it all meant the same thing.

We were caught.

"Crap," he said. "We have to go."

"What?"

"We have to go, Nic," he repeated. "They know we're guilty and there's no way I'm letting them take you into custody. They won't let us get away with this."

Well damn, I didn't even think about that outcome. Probably because it sounded like something you'd see in a James Bond film. This was Silverlake; there was nowhere we could hide that someone wouldn't find us. The world was closing in on us and with every tick of the grandfather clock in our living room I found it harder to breathe.

"So what are you suggesting?" I said, barely above a whisper.

"I'm saying we need to make a run for it," he replied. "Libby's right, we have to go now."

He grabbed the bag Libby had packed for me and popped the boot to his Lancer. Another larger bag was already sitting in there. Aiden looked questioningly at Libby.

"Noah packed a few of your things," she explained. "We figured you wouldn't have the time."

They were serious about this. I guess I couldn't really blame them. The reality of the situation was that we either go to jail or get out of town. No pressure. Was there a third option? My brain went haywire as I tried to think of some way I could explain this to the cops so we could just walk away.

The Mob killed Brooke, I killed Bobby in self-defence, we were blackmailed into the thefts … yeah, these facts might have been true but how could I explain about the Porsches I had helped steal? I couldn't think of any explanation for how we got into this—not one that anyone with a brain would believe anyway.

"Nic, I'm so sorry," Libby said quietly, interrupting my frantic thoughts. "You're right, this was all my fault." My guts clenched like they'd been kicked. Libby's eyes were full of guilt, but something else, too. Fear. My best friend was scared of me. What did that make me?

"No, Libby! It's not your fault. Forget I ever said that. Please!"

"Okay," she said weakly, but I knew there was no way she would ever forget it. It would always be between us.

Aiden stepped past me and enveloped Libby in a hug, muttering a thank you, and turned back to me.

"What do you say?" he asked. "Stay or go?"

Swallowing thickly, I looked between the two of them. This was my home, how was I supposed to just leave it all behind? I tried to imagine what would happen if I did leave. My parents would eventually come home from the bank and expect to see me come through the door after school. What would they do when I didn't? Would they worry so much that the lines on their forehead would stay etched deep in their skin? Or, would they hate me for what I did to my teachers? The police were on their way after all and, in a town like this, we were going to be found guilty no matter how good we were at covering ourselves. Despite my mastermind status, I just couldn't see how to talk my way out of this total shitstorm.

Honestly, even if we found a way to get out of this, I had still killed a man. The image of Bobby's body lying in the dirt would be burnt into my memory forever.

This town was going to be a constant reminder of the monster I was and I felt my throat close at the realisation. I couldn't stay here anymore. I couldn't be around my friends or family after what I did.

"Let's go."

Without hesitation, I grabbed Libby and wrapped my arms around her body in a desperate hug. I wanted her to come with us so badly and I would have asked but I knew that it wasn't possible. Right now, she wasn't in any trouble and if she came with us then we might as well have a massive banner announcing her involvement in the heist. She was safer staying behind.

"I guess this is goodbye then, loser," she said with a slight crack in her voice. I fought to keep my tears from spilling down my cheeks. Out of the corner of my eye I saw Aiden slipping into the house, giving us some privacy.

"This isn't goodbye, Libs," I said, letting go of her. "You're my best friend, I'll never say goodbye to you."

"Well, in that case," she said with a watery attempt at sarcasm, "I'll just see you later."

I wanted to tell her that nothing would change between us, that we would still be the dynamic duo, but who was I kidding? Even if I could stay, things wouldn't be the same between us. How could they? I wasn't even the same person I had been a few days ago.

I felt a huge part of my life slipping away, and I hugged her once more, tighter than ever before. I heard her sob into my shoulder.

"You're such a dork," I said gently.

"It takes one to know one," she quipped, wiping her face on her sleeve.

"Sorry to interrupt, ladies," Aiden chimed in, reappearing. "But we have to go now, Nic. We're running out of time."

We always seemed to be running out of time.

I squeezed her hand quickly and then climbed into the passenger seat. I barely had time to close the door before Aiden was throwing the car into reverse and flooring it down the street.

With one last glance out of the back window, I watched my home slowly disappear out of view.

* * *

The drive out of town was so tense that I felt like I was suffocating inside the car. The radio softly played some Paramore song I had never heard before and the wind whipped through our half open windows. Aiden stared intently at the road, deep in thought.

"Are you okay?"

He flicked his eyes towards me and gave a sad smile. "Are you?" he replied, returning his gaze to the road.

I inhaled and tried to steady my rapid heartbeat. I was scared of course. We were in serious trouble and there was no denying that. If the police caught up with us we were going to be in trouble with the law, but if Bobby's men caught up with us we were going to die.

My hands felt dirty as well. It was like Bobby's blood was permanently inked on them like a tattoo. I ended a person's life and no matter what would have happened if I didn't, I was still responsible for the death of Aiden's dad. They may not have had a normal father-son relationship, but Aiden must've had some kind of love for him. As twisted as it may have been.

Could he forgive me for what I did? Could anyone?

It's not like I'd be able to find out, we couldn't talk to our parents or our friends without putting them at risk and once the media found out about everything, our faces would be all over the country. The only person I had now was Aiden and all he had was me. I just hoped he could forgive me.

"I'm dealing," I replied, pausing for a moment. "I'm so sorry."

"Why?"

"For what I did to Bobby. I didn't want to but he was killing you. I just … please don't hate me."

"I could never hate you." The sincerity in his eyes was so thick that their usual darkness was almost non-existent. "I know my dad and he would have killed me. I would have done the same thing if he was choking you."

Was that supposed to cheer me up? I'm sure it was but all it did was cement the fact that I was becoming dark like Aiden. I suppose that was always going to be how it ended. You couldn't do bad things without changing who you were.

"Hey, I know it's a crap situation but we can make it work," he replied, changing lanes and weaving through the traffic. "We'll lay low for a while and wait until it all dies down."

He was making this sound like a holiday or something. Maybe the lack of air supply he suffered from the choking messed with his perception of reality. Or maybe that was just Aiden being Aiden.

Yep, probably option two.

"You know it's not that easy," I said, fiddling with the buttons for the air conditioning. "We have no idea where to go or what we are going to do. We'll need supplies and obviously money. We don't have anything."

"Actually we do."

My eyebrows knitted together and I turned to face him. His gaze was still on the road but he had a smirk on his bloodied face and a glint in his eyes.

"What did you do?" I knew him well enough by now to know that the look on his face meant nothing except trouble.

"I may or may not have taken some money from Dom's office before we left." His smirk grew wider. "She keeps her extra earnings in a locked drawer instead of taking it to the bank, so they don't get suspicious. It was incredibly easy to break into."

Seriously? I don't know if I was surprised that he had planned for this or that I wasn't all that shocked that he had. He had some kind of death wish or something.

"Are you crazy? She's not going to let that go, you know."

"She'll have to find us first," he replied nonchalantly. "Besides, it was rightfully mine. I brought in way more than I was paid for."

Unbelievable. I shook my head slightly and leaned back in my seat. There was no point in arguing over what was already done. To be honest, I was relieved that we were going to have enough money to keep us going for at least a while.

"How much did you take?"

"$20,000," he answered. "There's $10,000 left."

"Wait," I said. "How did you manage to spend $10,000 dollars in the last hour?" Was it the bruises on his face or did Aiden actually look a little shy?

"I left half at your parents' house just before we took off," he said. "Libby told me they were struggling. I thought since my grand plan of solving your money worries with the car heist didn't work out, I should, you know, leave a little something. Oh, I also picked up your mail while I was in the house." He pulled an envelope from the inside pocket of his leather jacket and put it on my lap, giving my leg a little squeeze.

Wow. Way too much to think about all at once. I was glad that Aiden had helped my parents, obviously, even though it was stolen money. Would that get them into trouble? And a little part of my brain, which I was trying to ignore, was thinking about the kind of money that was available to people once they put aside their worries about whether it was legal or moral—people like us. But mostly I was reeling from the idea that Aiden had thought he was getting me into this whole mess—*blackmailing* me into it, let's not forget—for my own good. This boy's ethics were all kinds of twisted. And I was going to have to deal with that.

"Thanks, I think," I finally managed to say. Aiden shrugged as if it was no big deal. I put the letter on the dashboard without even looking at it.

We pulled into a petrol station just off the highway.

"We need to make a stop for supplies and to fill the tank up."

I nodded and unbuckled my seatbelt. Aiden parked in front of a petrol pump and got out of the car, making his way to the boot. Opening it with a hard tug, he pulled out a small black camera bag that had been stuffed behind the spare tire. My eyes bulged when he unzipped it and I saw ten perfect little stacks of fifty dollar notes.

"Here." He handed me a few notes. "I'll fuel up if you want to grab the supplies."

Pocketing the money, I walked into the small store. The place wasn't anything special so we'd have to settle for a diet of junk food and energy drinks.

As I walked to the counter, I stopped when the small electronic stand caught my attention. On the top shelf were five plain black mobile phones and prepaid sim cards on sale.

Jackpot.

Our phones would be useless now that the police were searching for us. The sooner we dumped them, the safer we would be from being tracked. Anyone who owned a TV knew that phone tracing was the first step.

I quickly paid the cashier for the fuel and the supplies and walked back to the car. Aiden had already closed the fuel cap and started to load the bags into the boot.

"You know what the most ironic part about all of this is?" I said, leaning against his car. "We really are Bonnie and Clyde now. Who knew your fascination with crime couples would be spot on?"

He stood up straight and looked into my eyes. His own were filled with mischief and he had a playful smirk on his face.

"What?" I asked, wrinkling my face up slightly.

Without warning, he kissed me with a tenderness that made my body vibrate.

"That," he said with a chuckle. "I'm glad to have you as my Bonnie."

Not knowing what to do with myself, I leant forward to kiss him again. He was acting like none of this was even bothering him and maybe it wasn't. I knew that everyone dealt with things differently and maybe Aiden's way was to pretend nothing had even happened. I didn't know how he could; Aiden was just as much of a mystery now as he was before all of this.

He finished packing the boot and started the car.

"Where to now?" I asked

"Wherever we want to go, gorgeous," he replied, pulling out of the petrol station and merging onto the highway.

I noticed the letter I had discarded on the dashboard and picked it up. On the envelope was a logo that made my heart beat a little faster—Murdoch University. I ripped open the envelope. The first page was a standard letter sent to everyone who had registered their interest in Murdoch this year: applications for early admissions were now open, and I was invited to submit. The rest of the pages were the application form.

I looked up from the useless form and saw that we were driving past the exit sign for Silverlake. A surge of sadness hit me. I didn't need a guardian angel or a bad Christmas TV special to remind me what I could have had if I hadn't ruined everything. Maybe it was useless to dwell on what could have been, but my thoughts wouldn't allow anything else.

My life would have been beautiful. I would have spent four long but rewarding years at Murdoch before accepting an awesome journalism internship in Los Angeles. I would have spent the rest of my life with a partner who loved me for who I was and not what I was capable of. We would have lived near the beach and spent every Sunday lazing on the sand while the sun reflected upon the water. I would have grown old surrounded by my family and a career that would have made a difference in the world in some powerful way. I would have been happy.

Instead, I was running away with a guy who had dragged me into his messy life. I wasn't going to graduate and I definitely wasn't going to go to Murdoch. All I had left now was Aiden, and the thought made my throat close up in an attempt to stop myself from falling apart. After all the hours I had put into my Murdoch submission, I had ruined everything for a chance to prove myself, and for what? Just so I could end up being one of those girls who followed a guy wherever he went?

I was never going to have the future I wanted. Not now. It was ironic, really. I wanted nothing more than to get the hell out of this town and Murdoch was supposed to be my ticket. But now that I was really leaving, it felt wrong. That was poetic justice at its best. I wanted to get out so badly that I hadn't even considered it would mean saying goodbye to everything and everyone I knew. I got exactly what I wanted, just not in the way I had expected.

Without realising it, a few tears had started slipping from my eyes. I didn't stop myself this time.

"You okay?" Aiden asked, taking one of his hands off the wheel and lacing it with mine.

Even after everything he had done, I couldn't bring myself to hate him. There was no energy left in my body for hate, only for sadness.

"Yeah, I'm okay," I said with a watery smile. "Just thinking about Libby."

It was more than just her though. I was worried about my parents and what would happen to them now. What would they do when they found out about what we did? I crumpled the letter from Murdoch in my hand. I was leaving behind everyone who loved me, and my chance at a supposedly glittering academic career. Everything was such a mess now.

"Don't worry," he reassured me with a squeeze of my hand. "We'll be back."

I suppose he was right. One day we'd be back. We couldn't run forever and we both knew we'd return home eventually. After all, it was the only place we really knew. I had also promised Libby that I was never going to say goodbye to her and I meant it. Maybe we weren't the dynamic duo any more, but she would always be family to me.

I didn't know what Aiden and I were going to do now or where we were going to go. All I did know was that we were leaving our old lives behind in Silverlake and our next step was either going to be our salvation or our demise.

I could only hope that it was the first option.

Acknowledgements

You'd think after completing a novel, writing the acknowledgements would be easy. However, there has been so much love and support given to me over the years that I just don't know where to start. But here goes:

Thank you, Mum and Dad, for not only reminding me that I could make my dreams a reality but also for supplying me with copious amounts of frozen cokes and love during the dreaded editing stage.

Special thanks to my best friend of twelve years and partner-in-crime, Laura Williams, for being the Libby to my Nic. Without you, there wouldn't have been a story to begin with and I wouldn't have had the courage to write one.

Huge thank you to my FRamily: Nate, Tegs, Geoffy, Mark, and Kal, for being so supportive that they didn't even hesitate to stage a fake car chase just so I could be accurate in my descriptions. You have no idea just how much I appreciated the support and total lack of judgement.

Thank you, Jill Carnegie, for making sure that I always knew how special my words could be and for being the first editor and believer in this story. While I wish I could say thank you in person, I will have to settle for sharing my gratitude through these pages.

Special thank you to the ladies at the *Gold Coast Bulletin*, Amy Lane and Kelly Casey, for helping fifteen-year-old me nurture my writing abilities and for also accidentally introducing me to my publisher. Who knew mixing up book review requests would lead to such a wonderful outcome?

And finally, thank you to my publisher Michelle Lovi and the team at Odyssey Books for not only taking a chance on me but for also ensuring that my novel was in very good hands.

About the Author

Tasman Anderson is an Australian author, writer and award-winning journalist. She has written for the *Gold Coast Bulletin*, Youth Journalism International, *Q Magazine*, *Teen Voices* and *Loving Logan*. When she's not spending her time ignoring the sunlight and writing young adult fiction, she's most likely binging on Netflix and going on sushi dates with her best friends. *Know Your Enemy* is Tasman's first novel.

You can visit her at www.tasmananderson.com.